ROAD
to
BETHLEHEM

Reviewers Praise
The Seeds of Christianity Series

Witness is a love story, and a good one.
—Christy Award Winner, Jill Williamson

Mr. Lewis weaves the lore seamlessly into the adventure, blending meticulous research and practiced storytelling into a delightfully satisfying tale you won't soon forget.
—It Is To Write

Witness will keep you glued to your seat turning pages long into the night. And the characters are just wonderful! I love Rivkah and feel like she's family now! I highly, highly recommend his books. You will be moved by God and E.G. Lewis' writing as much as I was..I am sure of it!
—Michelle Vasquez

Author E. G. Lewis has a wonderful skill with his writing, hiding deep and serious research under simple, honest story-telling. There's no feel of being overwhelmed with teaching in *Disciple* — neither religious nor historical. To research so deeply and tread so lightly is a wonderful talent .
—Sheila Deeth

Witness is worthy of so much more than a 5 star rating. It's an emotional story full of fiction but also full of actual events...
—Molly Edwards

Lewis's writing is so provocative, so descriptive and in tune with the human psyche...He draws us with such craft and precision that before you know it you just have to keep reading.
—Tracy Krauss

Reviewers Praise
The Seeds of Christianity Series

This book, *Martyr*, delves into the humanity and depravity of both the Jewish and Roman peoples, medicine, the military and economics...and all with a bit of humor.　　　　—Tammy Litke

God, as depicted in *Apostle* is ever-present in the characters' lives, but never intrusive in the tale or the history.

　　　　　　　　　　　　　　　　　　　—Gregory Thomas

The true delight of The Seeds of Christianity is not just the great storyline, but the historical setting the author so brilliantly depicts. You feel the heat of the potter's kiln on your face and the cool of the wine grapes on your bare feet as everyday life in the ancient Middle East comes alive on each page.

　　　　　　　　　　　　　　　　　　　　—Bruce Judisch

It was a gripping story, not in a who-dun-it manner but rather in a way that made me want to learn what happened next, to be part of their story.

　　　　　　　　　　　　　　　　　　　—Wyndy Callahan

You will rejoice and cry at various times. These are novels that will transport you to a different world.

　　　　　　　　　　　　　　　　　　　—Isabelle Lusier

The author did a wonderful job on weaving history and fact together to make fast-paced and gripping books.

　　　　　　　　　　　　　　　　　　　—Sarah Bailey

Books by E. G. Lewis

The Seeds of Christianity™ Series

ROAD TO BETHLEHEM — *A Prelude*

WITNESS — Book One

DISCIPLE — Book Two

APOSTLE — Book Three

MARTYR — Book Four

The Mountain Memories Series

PROMISES — Book One

LOST — Book Two

Christian Non-Fiction

At Table with the Lord - Foods of the First Century

All Things Christmas - The History & Traditions of
Advent and Christmas

In Three Days - The History & Traditions of
Lent and Easter

About the Author

Writing has always been a major part of E. G Lewis' life. A former newspaper editor and publisher, his articles have appeared in many national and regional magazines. He also wrote and directed corporate training films.

He has a graduate degree in Economics from Ohio State University and worked in management and corporate planning before deciding to become a fulltime novelist. He and his wife, Gail, an editor and writer, live on the Southern Oregon Coast.

ROAD
To
BETHLEHEM

A Prelude to

The
Seeds of Christianity™ Series

A Novel

by

E. G. Lewis

Cape Arago Press
PO Box 771
North Bend, OR 97459
www.capearagopress.com

Published by Cape Arago Press
P.O. Box 771 North Bend, OR 97459

Cover: *Mary and Joseph Travel to Bethlehem at Sunset*
© Shutterstock, Inc.

ISBN 13: 978-0982594971
ISBN 10: 982594976

1. Fiction: Christian—Historical   2.Fiction: Christian—Biblical

As always, I want to offer my heartfelt thanks to all those who facilitated my research by graciously sharing their knowledge and expertise. They supported my goal of accurately depicting everyday life in the era during which Christianity came to be. Without their help, The Seeds of Christianity™ might never have germinated.

This book is dedicated with love and gratitude to my wife, and best friend, Gail. Throughout the Series, she has played an invaluable role.

Beautiful Lady, I couldn't have done it without you.

~ **1** ~

"And the man departed from the town of Bethlehem in Judah, to live where he could find a place..." ~ Judges 17:8

"Yours or mine?"

Tovit frowned and shrugged away any interest in the item. Two days of dividing the tools had taken its toll on both men.

Yosef dropped the chisel in his sack and resumed poking through the box. When he finished with the box, he slipped his hand into the back of a drawer and pulled out a package wrapped in a square of butter-soft deerskin. He loosed the hemp twine and removed a pair of brass calipers. Finely made, the tool had scrollwork on its arms and a knurled ivory handle at the top. He turned it over in his hand then carefully rewrapped it and placed it in his satchel.

"That stays.," Tovit said as he reached for the package. "It belongs to the shop."

Yosef grabbed his forearm, stopping him. His eyes were hard as flint when he faced his older brother. "It is mine."

"We need to discuss this."

"There is nothing to discuss. Abba gave me those calipers

when I moved up from apprentice to journeyman."

"They have been in the shop for as long as I can remember."

"So have I," Yosef said with a thin smile. He lifted Tovit's arm out of the satchel and tossed the strap over his shoulder. "I am taking this load out to the donkey."

Never one to concede a point easily, Tovit followed him. "Moving far from family makes no sense. Who will come to your aid if are injured or become ill?"

"This is a rare opportunity," Yosef replied over his shoulder. "How often is a man's son not interested in taking over his father's business? Surely you can see the hand of the Lord at work here." Yosef packed the tools into the donkey's basket and headed back to the shop.

Tovit trailed behind, dogging his steps. "The risk is too great. If this plan of yours does not work out, you will lose all that you have. Abandon this idea now before it is too late."

"It is already too late. Have you forgotten? I am leaving today." Yosef tried to stifle his grin.

Six weeks before, Yosef's merchant friend, Kahlil, dropped by the shop. During his visit Kahlil told him of the death of a carpenter in Nazareth. Yosef listened and nodded as he worked, pretending to be interested. Everything changed when he heard how eager the man's son was to dispose of his late father's estate.

Intrigued, Yosef made the journey to the Galilee. He looked at the small house with attached carpentry shop and negotiated the purchase then and there. He planned his relocation on the way back to Bethlehem.

As it turned out, his older brother, Tovit, was not keen on him leaving.

"Find a way to back out of the contract," his brother had said. "Stay here in Bethlehem; I need an assistant."

Tovit gritted his teeth. The words hadn't come out the way he intended. Instead of reminding Yosef of the steady work available in Bethlehem, he'd disparaged his abilities by referring to him as an *assistant*.

"It was kind of you to offer," Yosef said, overlooking his brother's gaffe. "But have you forgotten about Matthan? He will join you in the business before you know it."

"Let us not kid ourselves. Matthan is a *boy*, not yet qualified enough for me to even call him an apprentice. I have been trying to teach him a bit now and then just as our father brought us along, but we both know he is far from ready."

"We also both know Matthan grows older each and every day."

"Suppose you agreed to stay only until Matthan comes of age?" Tovit asked with unexpected enthusiasm.

"What will you do then? Inform your brother Yosef that you no longer have need of his services, or send your son away? My opportunity is here and now, not several years in the future."

Tovit continued following him back and forth, berating him as they walked. "Have you no heart? How can you go off on this adventure of yours and leave me without adequate help. Do you care nothing about what happens to me and my family? Who will do the work while Matthan grows into a man? Do not leave me like this."

Yosef stopped and spun around to face him. "*Leave you like this*? As the eldest son you received our father's blessing. You inherited his home and business as your birthright, forcing his other son, me, to go into the world and fend for himself."

Tovit tossed an empty palm into the air. "Neither of us made those rules. That's the way it has always been."

"And I have accepted that." Yosef gripped Tovit's shoulders and stared into his brother's eyes. "I do not begrudge you for what you received. In turn, all I ask is that you not disparage whatever small successes I stumble upon in this world."

Leaving Tovit beside the donkey, Yosef went inside to gather the last of his tools. Knowing he was leaving soon, Tovit's children surrounded their beloved uncle. They dabbed away tears as they said good-bye.

Galena, Tovit's wife, hugged him tightly and kissed his cheek. "You are a good man, Yosef. I pray you prosper in the Galilee. Spread your wings and soar like an eagle, but never forget to visit us when you return for the Festivals."

Yosef sighed. "If only your husband shared your sentiments."

She glanced back over her shoulder, making sure the children couldn't overhear. Leaning close, she whispered, "Tovit is afraid to have you leave. He fears his customers will go elsewhere if you are not here."

He gave her an indulgent smile. "Tovit afraid? Are these kind words intended to make me feel better? I find such a thing hard to believe."

"A man whispers things to his wife when they lie in bed at night that he would never utter in the light of day."

Yosef's brow wrinkled. "Why should he feel this way?"

"Because he has good reason to worry about you leaving."

"What you say makes no sense. Tovit has a fine reputation."

"True, Tovit has a fine reputation. Which is well and good as far as it goes. Yet sometimes the customer wants more than merely a utilitarian object. They seek a little something extra, an embellishment...a unique detail. To do that demands an artistry Tovit does not possess. Trust me, Yosef. You will be missed, *greatly* missed."

She caught his sleeve when he turned to leave. Shaking her head, she brought a finger to her lips. "It is in everyone's best interest that none of this reach Tovit's ear."

He nodded as he turned away. Yosef stored the last few items and untied the donkey's reins. The time had come for him to go.

The two brothers had spent their entire life working side-by-side, learning their father's trade. All those years, the good times and the not-so-good times, had come down to this final moment. Yosef looked over at his brother with love in his heart. He struggled to compress a lifetime's worth of memories and emotions into a few words. "Peace be upon you and your house. I will remember you before the Lord whenever I pray. *Kol Tuv*, my brother."

Tovit shocked him by spitting at his feet. "Keep your prayers and good wishes for yourself. You will need them more than I. Take your donkey and get out of my sight. I no longer have a brother."

Fear, anger and disappointment roiled within Tovit as he stood in the middle of the road. He rested his hands on his hips and watched the dust swirl in the breeze as Yosef trudged away.

Galena joined her husband in the road saying nothing. She waited until Yosef disappeared over a distant rise. Turning to face her husband, she said, "I hope you're pleased with yourself. Like Esau, your foolish temper has put your brother to flight."

~ 2 ~

"Pay to all what is due them: taxes to whom taxes are due, revenue to whom revenue is due, respect to whom respect is due, honor to whom honor is due." ~ Romans 13:7

Yosef arrived in Nazareth four days later. He unloaded his cargo, certain that the donkey gave a sigh of relief each time he removed more weight. He led the animal around to the back of the house and removed his reins and bit. After making a quick check of the fence to verify its ability to contain the animal, he filled the water trough, bolted the gate and left him to graze.

He returned to the front of the building and hauled his tools into the workshop. He stacked them along the workbench and shelves, sorting them in general groups. The hammers went in one clump, saws in another, and planes and chisels in another. He was debating how much work he should do in the shop when fatigue convinced him to put it off until the following day.

Seduced by an opportunity he felt too great to pass up, Yosef had given the house little consideration. He inwardly groaned as he glanced around the modest house that'd sat unoccupied for months. He found a pile of splintery wood in one corner of the room. Raising his eyes, he noticed sunlight coming through the roof.

It was a familiar sequence, one he knew well. The roof had leaked during the rainy season, probably not for the first time. The wet sheathing gradually rotted and collapsed onto the floor below. He made a mental list of what it would take to fix the damage. Tear back the roof, check the joists, replace the sheathing, haul fresh clay up to the roof, cover the repair and roll it smooth.

Dusty cloths covered the odd pieces of furniture abandoned when Ebenezer's widow went to reside with their son. Cabinet doors stood ajar. Webs dangled from the forgotten crocks and bowls littering the kitchen counters. He shook his head, imagining the labor required to make this neglected home habitable again.

Yosef carried his bedroll into the house, selected the cleanest corner, and unrolled it. He tossed his traveling cloak onto a shrouded piece of furniture and promised to deal with it in the morning. He sat cross-legged on the floor and supped on the remains of the midday meal he'd purchased in Nain. Then he washed and collapsed into bed, falling asleep while completing his evening prayers.

Normally an early riser, Yosef didn't stir again until mid-morning. He spent his first day in Nazareth moving about in a fog as he tried to prioritize the myriad tasks that needed doing.

After several days of recuperation, Yosef harnessed the donkey and loaded up the essential tools of his trade. By the end of the day he was in the village of Yotapata finalizing the details of the work he would perform in exchange for a defunct carpentry shop in Nazareth.

It took Yosef a little over two months to complete his indentured servitude to Ebenezer's son. As agreed, he added two rooms to the son's home to provide living space for his mother. He made other repairs to the main structure as well, and built furniture for the widow.

Having worked off his debt, he returned to Nazareth a free man. He found himself humming Psalms as he walked and greeting passersby with a smile and a friendly wave. Why shouldn't he be happy? Yosef thought. Fortune had smiled on him.

He was heading *home*. Home to Nazareth and a business that was his own. Just thinking about it filled him with an invigorating sense of optimism. He was realistic enough to know that establishing any new business would take both time and effort. He had nothing but time and had always been a hard worker.

Upon his return from Yotapa, Yosef went to the synagogue every *Shabbat* and began to make friends. The residents of Nazareth were delighted at the thought of having a local carpentry shop again.

After he'd completed the most pressing repairs to his home and shop, he officially opened for business. He found that occupying *the house of the carpenter* brought a certain amount of business to his door. Especially in a town that had been without a carpenter for nearly six months. He'd been open only a few days when the townspeople started trickling in seeking repairs for broken or damaged items.

Others placed orders for small household items. He understood they were limiting their risk while testing the skill and prices of the new man in town. Even though he earned little profit on these transactions, he welcomed the opportunity to make their acquaintance.

Just as in Bethlehem, Yosef tallied his earnings on the last day of each week and marked the sum on a board with a piece of charcoal. This ritual was his way of preparing for the *Shabbat* by determining the week's tithe.

While he still had the coins there on the table in front of him he reached into a drawer and removed a squat jar emblazoned with the Hebrew letter *Shin*. He'd asked the potter to imprint the *Shin* on the outside before he fired it to symbolize *El Shaddai*, God Almighty. Removing the cork, he scooped up an amount equal to his tithe and trickled the coins into the neck of jar. This was his second tithe, funds he would spend when in Jerusalem for the pilgrim Festivals of *Pesach, Shavu'ot* and *Sukkoth*.

He also set some aside for the coming week's tolls and taxes, a cost of doing business in the Roman Empire. Yosef stared at the pitiful pile of coins remaining on the table and shook his head. He picked up his tally board, sighing as he ran his eyes down the column of figures. Business was not increasing as he'd hoped it would. As a matter of fact, there were several weeks when it actually declined.

Some weeks he barely had enough left over to buy food. He still had most of the money he brought with him from Bethlehem, and was glad for it. But that had to go for materials and supplies. When he exhausted his savings, he didn't know what he'd do. For the first time since he'd started down this heady path to independence, Yosef recalled Tovit's ominous warnings.

Could Tovit have been correct?

~ 3 ~

"My soul yearns for thee in the night, my spirit within me earnestly seeks thee." ~ Isaiah 26:9

"We could loll in the shade and watch the fishing boats glide across the water." Anak gave a contented stretch and faked a yawn. "For the last time, are you coming with us tomorrow?"

Yosef made another a long stroke with the plane and shook his head. "Also for the last time, I have deadlines to meet. I cannot walk away and leave my work undone."

Anak shrugged. "Let your customers wait."

"But I told them their orders would be ready."

"Will the mountains collapse into the sea if they do not get them on time? Come with us. You work too hard, take a little rest."

"Like the Lord God, I work six days and rest on the seventh... the *Shabbat*."

"All we can do on the *Shabbat* is go to the synagogue and then stay at home. Where is the fun in that?"

"I gave the customers my word."

"Did the rabbi attest to your agreement?"

Yosef scoffed. "Of course not, it was an everyday business transaction."

Anak wandered about the cluttered workshop, stopping here and there to poke around. He reached up and rattled the saws dangling from a ceiling joist as he passed. "Then why worry? They cannot accuse you in front of the elders of the synagogue. Besides, how can they complain if you are not here to listen?"

Yosef gave him a wry look. "I am beginning to see how the snake managed to convince Eve it would be a good thing to eat the fruit."

Scooping up a handful of wood curls off the workbench, Anak tossed them into the air. He made a great show of fanning away the dust. "Working amidst all this wood dust has clouded your judgment."

He planted his elbows on the workbench and stared into Yosef's eyes. "There is more to life than work, my friend. Fresh sea air is the antidote. You left Bethlehem and came to Nazareth so you could be nearer to the sea. What good is it if you never go there and enjoy it?"

"Stick to the truth. I left Bethlehem last year because my older brother had already married and taken over the family business after our father died. He had a son coming on and Bethlehem could not support a third carpenter. If I wanted to have my own shop, I had to leave. I chose to come here because I heard that Nazareth had lost its carpenter. I bought the business from his son to be close to Sepphoris, *not* the Lake of Gennesareth."

He squinted at the board in the vise before giving it a final swipe with the plane. "Not that I would ever live in Sepphoris," he said as he worked. "It is a thoroughly Roman city with baths and theatres. It even has a coliseum where they hold games, certainly no place for an observant Jew."

"I see. So you have a commitment in Sepphoris tomorrow?"

"No. I will be right here in my shop doing what I am doing now, working."

Anak thumped his fist on the corner of the workbench. "How many times must I tell you? The work will be waiting here when you return."

"And my unhappy customers will be waiting as well." Yosef loosened the vise, flipped the board over and re-tightened it. "Unlike some people whose money grows on trees, I earn my living making things. I shall invite you to go to the seashore in the middle of the olive harvest. See who begs off then."

Anak opened his mouth to respond, but stopped when someone softly tapped on the workshop door.

A young woman popped her head in and glanced around. Seeing Yosef behind his workbench, she smiled and entered the shop. "*Shalom Aleichem*. I hope I am not interrupting. You must be Yosef, the new carpenter from Judea. My mother asked me to see if the stool she ordered is ready."

"Anna, the wife of Yoachim?" Yosef asked as he strode across the room brushing curls of wood from his muscular forearms.

The young woman nodded. "Yes, Anna is my mother. I am called Miryam."

Yosef's dark eyes sparkled when he smiled. "*Aleichem Shalom, Miryam*. I am pleased to make your acquaintance." He removed a light colored stool from beneath a shelf on the far wall and brought it to her.

Miryam sat down the basket she carried and studied the stool he'd set before her. Her eyes widened the longer she examined it.

"I hope it is satisfactory," Yosef said as he watched her reaction. "Your mother simply ordered a milking stool. She didn't specify any details, so I let the wood tell me what it wanted to be."

"Satisfactory? Oh, it is more than satisfactory, far more. It is lovely. You turned a utilitarian object into a work of art. Imma will be pleased beyond measure." Miryam smiled. "I hope you enjoy making stools. When Imma's friends see this, they will be lined up at your door wanting one like it."

Yosef dipped his head in acknowledgement.

Miryam swept her skirt around her and sat on the stool. She leaned one way and another, testing its height and stability. She glanced up at him and grinned. "It is perfect. I shall feel like a princess every time I milk the goats."

"It is just a stool," he mumbled as he smoothed his beard and straightened his tunic.

"You would not say that if you saw the splintery thing I had been using. It was nothing but a slice of tree with some legs jammed into it." She ran a fingertip across the seat. "Instead of being smoothed and polished like this, it still had bark around its edge. I whispered a prayer of thanksgiving when Abba tossed it into the fire."

She gave him several coins in payment. "You certainly deserve more, but this is all Imma gave me."

"There is no need to apologize. It is what we agreed upon."

After he'd pocketed the money, she offered him the basket covered with a napkin. "Imma also sent some honey cakes." Miryam lowered eyes. "She said a man living alone does not get many sweets."

When she turned to leave, Yosef quickly stepped around her and pulled the door back. He smiled down at her as she crossed the threshold in front of him. "Tell your mother I send my thanks. May *HaShem* bless you both."

Resting an elbow against the doorjamb, he lingered in the doorway. A pleasant smile slowly curled his lips as he watched Miryam cross the village square with her new stool. Yosef had just found something he'd been looking for all his life. When she disappeared from view, he turned away and closed the door with a sigh.

Anak had remained slouched against the back wall with arms folded across his chest throughout the transaction. He noted the way Yosef tenderly carried the basket into the house before returning to his workbench.

Yosef picked up his plane and glanced back at his friend. "Why the face?"

"Why indeed? I saw the way you looked at her." He extended his arm and dangled his fingers. "My name is Miryam and I brought a basket of honey cakes for the skilled artisan," he mimicked in a lilting falsetto as he tiptoed in a circle.

Approaching the workbench, Anak slapped his friend on the back. "Are you certain it is only your work that keeps you here in town?" he asked with a manly chuckle. "You are still new to Nazareth so let me give you a word of caution concerning Miryam. Though she is certainly an attractive young woman, I suggest you tread cautiously. She is a bit too religious for some people's taste."

"Meaning you?"

"Me," Anak said with a nod, "and many others."

"You make it sound like a bad thing. How can a woman be too religious? Charm is deceitful, and beauty is vain, but a woman who fears the Lord deserves to be praised."

"Did your father never have a talk with you about women?"

"I am not a child. I know everything a man needs to know about women."

Anak inched closer and lowered his voice to a conspiratorial tone. "All I am saying is a *little* religion is a nice thing to have in a wife. It gives them something to think about, makes them less irritable and more sociable."

He raised his hand and brought his thumb and forefinger close together. "But just a wee bit, only a pinch. When a woman becomes overly religious she loses interest in certain *other* wifely obligations." He elbowed him in the ribs. "If you know what I mean. After all, David surely did not marry Bathsheba so they could spend their evenings reading the Torah together, now did he?"

"Despite what you imagine, a virtuous wife is more valuable than a house or riches. Houses and wealth you can inherit from your father, but a holy wife is from the Lord." Yosef picked up his chisel and mallet. "Now get out of here. I have work to do."

~ 4 ~

"They are made by carpenters...they can be nothing but what the artisans wish them to be."
                              ~ The Epistle of Jeremiah, Baruch 6:45

His search for additional sources of income led Yosef to nearby Sepphoris, the Capital of the Galilean region. In addition to various Roman officials and functionaries, it was also home to a number of affluent merchants and traders. He hoped to secure more profitable commissions by letting these powerful individuals know of his skills and abilities.

He started spending one or more days each week in Sepphoris. With the strap of his tool box slung over his shoulder, he crisscrossed the forum introducing himself to potential customers. He wanted everyone to know about the new carpenter in nearby Nazareth.

After several fruitless trips, a chain of events created the opportunity he'd been waiting for. Yosef was crossing the forum when the axle holding the wheel of a slave's overburdened wheelbarrow split in two. The cart's front end immediately crashed to the ground, nearly sending the slave flying over it.

The wheel, meanwhile, celebrated its freedom by zipping across the open square. Yosef saw the renegade circle of wood heading toward him and stuck out his foot. The wheel bounced off his sandal, made several wobbly circles then collapsed. He picked it up and carried it back to where it came from.

He found the harried slave on his hands and knees, scrambling to gather up the spilled produce. All the while his Master's chef berated him for such ineptitude on the day of a great banquet.

"It is hardly fair to blame him," Yosef said as he came up behind them. "Had the cart not been overloaded, the axle would surely have gotten you home."

The chef whirled around. "Who are you?"

"A carpenter from Nazareth, and I believe this is yours." He handed the man the wheel. "Allow me to take a look at the wheelbarrow. Perhaps I can fix it well enough to get you and your provisions home in time to prepare your Master's meal."

The chef handed the wheel back to him and resumed muttering as he picked through the load, assessing the damage.

Ignoring him, Yosef squatted to examine the cart. He wiggled one side of the splintered axle back and forth until he could free it. "I will be back in a few moments," he said and left with the piece of axle in his hand.

He went to the seller of doves and pigeons and asked to see one of his perches. After comparing the square rod to the axle's diameter, he asked to buy two perches and a length of cage wire.

Returning to the wheelbarrow, he cut both perches in half and stacked the four pieces together, forming a square. He tightly wrapped wire around one side before rounding the edges to the proper diameter. Flipping this temporary axle on end, he slid the wheel down to the center and wired the other side of the axle together. Next, he laid this new *axle* over the wheelbarrow's front arms and cut it to size.

He shaved down the ends to fit the holes left by the old axle and fit them into place. For reinforcement, he ran a double strand of wire across wheelbarrow's front arms. Inserting a metal tool, he twisted them together, locking the new axle in place.

"There, that should get you home safely," Yosef said, dusting his hands. The chef offered him payment, but he shook his head. "I was glad to help. I am here the third day of each week, think of me when you have need of a carpenter." He threw the strap on his toolbox over his shoulder and sent them on their way.

Less than an hour later the city's shoppers parted to let a slave-borne litter enter the forum. A short, balding man in a cloak edged in purple exited the litter and strode to the center of the plaza. He stopped beside a life-sized statue in the center of the plaza honoring Mercury as patron of financial gain and commerce.

Too short to see over the customer's heads, the man clambered onto the circular base of the large statue. He looped his elbow over Mercury's extended forearm for balance and scanned the crowd. He smiled when he spotted a tall, bearded man with a toolbox hanging at his side.

Hopping down, the man shoved his way through the shoppers to get to Yosef. "Are you the *carpentarius* who repaired the slave's cart earlier this morning?"

Yosef acknowledged that he was indeed the one who'd fixed it.

The man identified himself as Brucius, Chief Steward of the City's Magistrate, Valerius Fabianus. "Do you also do interior work such as cabinetry?"

Yosef nodded.

"Good, I may have some work for you." Resting a hand on Yosef's shoulder, the man directed his attention to a large *villa* perched on a hill overlooking the city. "That is Fabianus' residence. His wife, Drusilla, wants to have a new cabinet made and he's seeking a *carpentarius* to build it for her. Meet with me tomorrow morning and we can discuss the details."

Yosef entered Sepphoris at first light. Tired from the long walk, but invigorated by the potential of a profitable commission, he cut a diagonal path across the forum. Rows of stalls were already popping up in the city's central marketplace. The sound of multiple voices buzzed around him as the merchants prepared for the day's customers.

Wisps of smoke rose from a row of braziers as a man in a heavy leather apron kindled his fires. A nearby table held pans of marinade and skewered meat in anticipation of hungry shoppers. Across the aisle, skins of wine hung in the shade beneath the wine seller's awning.

Following the directions Brucius gave him the previous day, Yosef made a turn at the Temple dedicated to the cult of Vulcan and Vesta. The road led him out of the city and past vineyards and olive groves. It terminated at a lane with an ornate wrought iron gate across its entrance.

A bell jingled when he tugged a rope.

A gatekeeper emerged from a small hut, stretched and asked his name. Yosef identified himself and his mission. The Steward had already alerted the gatekeeper of Yosef's impending visit. The man swung back the gate and motioned him through. The access road curved its way around and up the hillside. The curves reduced its grade, making it easier for horses pulling carriages or wagons.

Pressed gravel crunched under Yosef's sandals as he walked. The wispy remnants of the overnight fog gradually disappeared as he neared the top of the hill. Still low in the sky, the early morning sun cast long, dewy shadows over the grounds.

Fabianus' estate displayed the best in Roman art and architecture. Rows of privet bounded the perimeter of the upper drive on both sides. Old and dense, the hedge was trimmed to waist height. The limestone facade on the front of the building gleamed bright white and a row of arched windows, curtained against the sun, ran across the front wall.

The home's terracotta roof extended over the main entrance to a pair of pillars, creating a portico. Wide patios with marble railing, benches and small trees in planters jutted out from both sides of the expansive *domus*. A soft breeze refreshed Yosef as he climbed the half dozen steps to the entrance.

A doorman admitted him when he knocked. He led Yosef around an indoor fountain in the center of the *vestibulum* and down a long hallway with paneled frescoes on both sides. They came to a stop in front of a pair of tall oak doors. When the doorman knocked, a voice inside bid them enter.

Brucius looked up from his table. "It is good to see you again. Fabianus would like to discuss the project with you personally. I will take you to him," he said as he rose.

~ 5 ~

"The memory...like a blending of incense prepared by the art of the perfumer..." ~ Sirach 49:1

"It should be about this high and perhaps this wide." Fabianus sketched out the dimensions with his hands as he spoke.

Yosef mimicked his movements, making certain they understood each other. "Approximately this wide and this high? What is your wife planning on storing in it?"

Fabianus frowned when a slave appeared in the doorway. "Tell him to wait," he said, and waved the slave away before the man could say a word. "It is a *cabinet*. She can put whatever she likes in it. I have told its size, why should it matter to you what she wishes to place inside?"

"A gown or a cloak requires a deeper cabinet than a veil," Yosef replied with a calming smile. "Cabinets also generally have *three* dimensions. So far you have only specified two. Perhaps she wishes to use it for her cosmetics. In that case, it would be thin and require shelves."

"Details, details, details." Fabianus shook his head. "Her pestering over this cabinet has exhausted me. I am a busy man. Build it any way you like. I simply want it over and done with."

"Perhaps I should to speak to your wife since she is the one who will be using the cabinet."

"That is a marvelous idea." Fabianus caught the attention of a passing slave. "Take this man to see your mistress." Returning to his desk with a happy smile, he began shuffling through dispatches. "I cannot spend my day fussing over cabinets when there is work to be done."

Yosef thanked him for his time and followed the slave out of the room.

"Do not bother to check back with me," Fabianus called after him as they left. "Give her whatever she wants. Do a good job and my Steward will see that you are amply rewarded for your efforts."

The cabinet underwent extensive changes when Yosef consulted with Drusilla. "Whatever was Fabianus thinking? I have told him again and again I need a place to store my scarves and jewelry. I want it to be accessible. It should hang on the wall, not stand on the floor."

"Where will this cabinet go?" Yosef asked once they'd finalized the dimensions and construction details."

"In the alcove of my bedchamber, where I dress."

"If you would not mind showing me, I can try to match the wood and exterior stain to the other furniture in the room."

Crossing the hall, she pointed to an empty space between a pair of closets. "There."

Yosef studied the tone of their doors and made some notes for later reference. "I can make the cabinet of oak to match the closets. After I mix up a batch of stain, I will bring a sample for you to approve before applying it to the wood. It is the custom to line such cabinets with aromatic wood to repel moths and other insects. Have you considered this?"

She grimaced. "You are beginning to sound like my husband. I suppose you are now planning to insist that my cabinet must have Lebanon cedar on its interior."

Reading her body language, Yosef smiled and said, "Only if that is what you wish."

"What I do *not* want is to go to a dinner party with my scarf smelling like I just stepped out of a forest."

"I see." Yosef stroked his neatly-trimmed beard as he weighed his options. "I have an alternative to suggest, but first I must go into the marketplace for a sample."

Drusilla gave a dramatic sigh. "Very well, go if you must."

Leaving the home, Yosef hurried down the steps and jogged across the wide drive. Telling the gatekeeper he'd be right back, he headed for the forum. It took him only a few minutes to find the booths of the sellers of incense and perfumes. He asked one of the perfumers to dab a tiny amount of algum wood oil on a piece cloth. He tightly folded the cloth, tossed the woman a small coin and hurried back.

He found Camilla, Drusilla's chief handmaiden, sitting near the fountain waiting for him. She rose from the bench when Yosef came through the tall entry doors and crossed the *vestibulum* to meet him. "Good day, Yosef the *carpentarius*," she said. "*Domina* is relaxing in the conservatory. I will take you to her."

Yosef fell into step behind the woman. The semi-circular rotunda covering the *vestibulum* magnified the sound of their footsteps tapping across the Corinthian marble floor. Taking a side hallway, Camilla led him to a room off of the back of the house. It had rows of windows on all three walls. Exotic plants and flowers bloomed in profusion.

The heat and humidity of the solarium made a *stola* unnecessary. Drusilla reclined on a curved couch in a sleeveless robin's egg blue tunic. Over it she wore a white *palla*, or shawl, made of the sheerest silk. She'd pushed it back off of her shoulders, leaving it loosely draped about her. A slave sat at her feet on the flagstone floor strumming a *cithara*.

She glanced up when the door opened and smiled. "You are very prompt, Yosef. That is an admirable trait in a craftsman."

Camilla pulled a chair over beside the couch and Yosef sat. The musician retreated to a corner with his instrument. He stared out the window, pretending not to listen to their conversation.

"What have you brought me?"

"A cloth infused with the scent of algum wood so you may decide if it would be a satisfactory substitute for the cedar." Yosef carefully unfolded the swatch of cloth and handed it to her.

Drusilla passed it in front of her face and inhaled. She straightened on the couch and sniffed again. "What a wonderful scent it has. It is warm, soft, smooth...almost indescribable." She cocked her head and studied him. "You are clearly a man who understands a woman's heart."

He cleared his throat and admired the pattern of the floor.

She noticed and laughed. "Do not be embarrassed to receive such a compliment. Women appreciate a man who understands their needs and desires. So there truly is a wood that smells this wonderful?"

"Indeed there is. Today, I brought you a few drops of the oil they extract from this wood. The heartwood retains its fragrance so algum wood emits this pleasant aroma for several decades."

"This is an inspired choice." She gave an excited shiver. "I can hardly wait to see my new cabinet."

"I will have to see if the wood merchant has any algum wood in stock. It can be costly, so he limits the amount he buys."

"But I must have it," she said with a pouty frown. "What will we do if this man has none for sale?"

"My people have a saying, 'Good things come to those who wait.' Algum wood comes from far off. Fortunately, this time of year there are ships from Ophir arriving at the Red Sea port of Berenike every few days. It should not take him overly long to secure the wood I require. In the meantime, I will begin work on the cabinet itself."

"Brucius was right to speak highly of you." Drusilla unexpectedly reached out and squeezed his hand. "You seem to know how much this means to me. I shall place this matter in your competent hands and trust you will not disappoint me."

Her eyes narrowed. "Never forget, my husband is a *very* powerful man."

~ 6 ~

"Moreover the servants of Huram and the servants of Solomon,
who brought gold from Ophir, brought algum wood..."

~ 2 Chronicles 9:11

Yosef left his work and hurried to the door when he heard frantic pounding. He was surprised to find Miryam on the other side. Tears glistened in her eyes.

"What has happened to upset you so?"

"I had a terrible accident."

He opened the door wide and motioned her into his workshop. "Are you injured? Should I send for a physician?"

A weak smile crossed her lips and just as quickly disappeared. "No, no. It is nothing like that." She adjusted her veil and brushed an arm across her brow. "I ran all the way and need to catch my breath."

"Come, sit down and rest for a few moments. I will pour you some water."

She sipped the water then took a deep breath, releasing it slowly. "I do not know what I would have done if you had not been here. You are the only one who can possibly help me."

He swept aside the tools and placed the flat of his hands on his workbench. "Tell me how I can help you solve this problem of yours."

Miryam reached into the soft-sided market basket she carried and extracted a handful of wood. "This is my problem," she said, placing the pile of scrapes in front of him.

"It is, or at least it was, a wooden box," Yosef said while he sorted through the parts. "Well made, probably quite lovely. Something a woman might use for special items such as pins or jewelry" He turned one of the pieces in hand. "The joinery differs from what I usually see. It could be foreign made."

"My grandfather purchased the box from a traveling merchant as a gift for my grandmother. It became Imma's when Savta died. I was dusting this morning and did not see it on the table. It crashed to the floor when I bumped it with my hand. I went over to pick it up and it was as you see it now," she dabbed at her eye, "all in pieces."

He picked up a long rectangular piece with a splintered edge. "One of the pieces, the bottom, split in half when it hit the floor." He raised his eyebrows in a gesture of hopelessness. "Without the bottom to hold things together, everything went its own way."

Picking up the lid, Yosef leaned toward the open window. He held the piece in the sunlight and examined it carefully. "There are a few minor nicks on the lid, but a little stain and beeswax polish will easily hide them. The sides also seem to have survived undamaged."

His confident manner acted like a healing balm, calming her anxieties. Miryam relaxed for the first time. "Will you be able to put it back together?"

"I believe so." He continued turning the wood back and forth in the sunlight. "The first thing I must do is determine what type of wood this is so I can try to match it." He spoke as much to himself as to her.

"Oh, that is easy. The merchant told Saba it was made of algum wood." A look of terror crept across her face. "What was I thinking? This is worse than anything I imagined. Solomon had to send all the way to Ophir to secure algum wood for his Temple. It is the wood of Kings, not normal people like you and me." She buried her face in her hands. "Imma will be heartbroken when she sees what I have done."

Knitting his brow in concentration, Yosef sniffed several of the pieces. He moved them this way and that like a dog trying to locate a scent.

Miryam's face registered her surprise as she watched. "What are you doing?"

"Testing the wood. It is, as you said, algum wood and quite old. The exterior has been exposed to the air for so many years that it no longer exudes the wood's characteristic aroma." He turned a piece in his hand and pointed. "But inside, down here where the pieces were joined, the scent can still be found."

He offered the piece to her. "Next to the joint, try it."

She held it close and breathed in. At first, she detected nothing then the subtle smell of the wood gradually came through. "Smelling it takes me back to when I was a very small child. I had forgotten how nice it was. " She closed her hands over it and pressed it to her bosom, "I am not sure I want to give it back," she said with a playful giggle.

An instant later a frown replaced her smile. "By proving it is algum wood, you also confirmed I must tell Imma that my carelessness destroyed her heirloom forever."

"Do not give up so easily."

"I see no reason for optimism here; we cannot go to Ophir."

"Let me look in my storehouse. What I find may surprise you." Yosef spread his long fingers and measured the broken piece. He rose and crossed the room. He paused at the narrow doorway to glance back at her. "I store my wood out here in a shed beside the house. You may come along if you wish," he said, lifting the bar.

Miryam stopped at the storehouse doorway. The room lay in near total darkness.

Undeterred, Yosef strode through the inky shadows like a cat on a moonless night. Walking by memory, he wove between the dark piles scattered about the floor. He grabbed a rope dangling from above and jerked it. Sunlight flooded in as the outside door swung aside.

Neat stacks of various types and sizes of wood were arranged on rows of raised pallets on the floor. Longer boards rested on wooden arms extending from both walls. Miryam watched Yosef move in and around the pallets and realized that what she'd first judged to be haphazard clutter was actually an ordered arrangement.

"I keep the doors shut because sunlight bleaches the wood," he explained as he poked amid the boards. He pointed to the wall beside him. "These boards are freshly cut. I open the vents on foggy nights to bring in moist air. It keeps them from drying too quickly and splitting."

Dropping to his knees beside a pallet, he began rummaging through the stack. He measured a board against the span of his fingers. He held it up for her to see. "Here it is."

"What is it," she asked from the doorway.

"I will let you tell me after you have smelled it," he said and handed her the board.

"How do you happen to have something as rare as algum wood in your storehouse?" Miryam asked as she watched Yosef prepare for work.

"It is expensive, but not rare. Trading ships from Ophir regularly arrive at the port of Berenike in Egypt. They transport exotic spices and other trade goods such as algum wood. The products go inland by caravan where they are loaded on barges and taken to Alexandria. From there they are distributed throughout the Roman Empire."

Setting the lid aside, Yosef began re-assembling the sides of the box into an open rectangle. "A few months ago, a wealthy customer in Sepphoris asked me to make a cabinet for his wife. She wanted it lined with algum wood since she planned to store her scarves in it. I ordered a little extra from the wood merchant." He rocked his hand in the air, "Just to be certain I would have enough."

"And you saved the leftover wood for me."

"Yes, I suppose I did, though I did not know it at the time. I save the scraps from every job. My storehouse may be as jumbled as Noah's Ark, but even the tiniest piece will make a pin." He lifted his eyes. "I am sorry. You must find all this talk of wood and carpentry boring."

"Not at all. Watching you work is fascinating...all your special tools and techniques. You are truly a skilled artisan." Miryam hesitated for a moment, nibbling her lip. "Uh, how long do you think it will take to repair the damage I caused?"

"It will not be ready this afternoon. After I cut and fit a new piece for the bottom, I will have to re-glue the joints. I am afraid there is no way you can slip in the new box and hope your mother does not notice."

"Oh, I would never try to deceive Imma. After I apologize for my daydreaming, I would like to tell her when it will be ready."

"I should have it finished by the day of preparation. That way she will have the entire *Shabbat* to enjoy it. Satisfactory?"

Miryam smiled and nodded.

Reaching into his tool kit, Yosef extracted a straight stick of hardwood fit through a mortise in a small block of wood. A thumb screw on top of the sliding block allowed the user to set its width. He placed the marking gauge across the box, snugged up the block, and secured it.

Moving to the piece of algum wood, he transferred the width of the box Miryam brought him to it. He returned to the box and repeated the process, recording its length this time. With the dimensions marked off, he clamped the wood and sawed it to size. When he finished, Yosef gathered up the sawdust. He rolled it up in a small cloth and handed it to her.

"This evening, before you tell your mother about the accident, place the sawdust in a bowl with a lit taper. Algum wood makes pleasing incense when it smolders." He winked. "Perhaps it will soften the blow."

Miryam sighed and stared at the floor. "There is something I should have told you before you started your work. I have no money to pay you. But I could work for you," she quickly added. "I am strong and healthy. I can carry wood, or sweep and cook and clean. That is, if you trust me not to destroy your things."

Placing his hand over hers, Yosef smiled and shook his head. "There is no need for you to do anything. Your visits are payment enough. As you said, I saved the leftover wood for you. I am happy I could be of assistance."

~ 7 ~

"...the lampstand also for the light, with its utensils and its lamps, and the oil for the light" ~ Exodus 35:14

Morning dew dampened Yosef's feet as he followed the grass path between the rows of olive trees. Pickers, day laborers hired for the harvest, moved among the branches on both sides of him as he walked.

The men had begun their day at sunrise by throwing the straps of a large sack over their shoulder. Moving into the grove, they propped rickety ladders against the trees and scaled them to gather the crop. They stretched this way and that, combing a boxlike device with teeth at one end through the branches while holding on for dear life with the other hand.

Every sweep of the harvester's arm dislodged olives and captured them in the box as they came off the tree. The pickers emptied the olives into their sack after each pass. When the sack was full, they tied the top and put it out on the grass path. Other workers periodically walked the rows, gathering the sacks and transporting them to the crushing room.

Anak saw Yosef coming with his toolbox dangling from a strap over his shoulder and raced out to meet him. "It is about time you got here. I had given up all hope of ever seeing you."

"Your messenger pounded on my door only minutes ago. I put aside everything and came right away. What constitutes such a *great emergency?*"

"Come," Anak motioned for him to follow, "come and I will show you."

Yosef followed him into a large barn built into the bank of a hillside. Crates of amphorae of various sizes were stacked in every available space. The two men threaded single file along a narrow, twisting route between the cases.

Reaching the far side of the warehouse, Anak opened a door

to the crushing room. "Look at this!" he wailed, pointing to the cracked and splintered end of a long wooden pole. "What are you going to do about this?"

Yosef shrugged. "Olives are your business, not mine. I planned to spend the day enjoying the beach at Lake Gennesareth."

"Even if that is a joke, it is not funny. Do you know anything about making olive oil?"

Yosef squatted and examined the rusty wire wrapped around an old fracture in the shaft. "Apparently more than you know about carpentry. When did this happen?"

"I came in to check the machinery this morning. I tried to turn the press by hand, but the wood broke apart instead of moving."

"I see." Yosef stroked his beard as he assessed the situation. "And you last used it when?"

Anak seemed surprised by the question. "Olives are always harvested in the month of *Tishri*. We finished pressing a year ago."

"So it has sat for a year. When did you decide to press this year's crop?"

Anak waved his arms and rolled his eyes. "There was nothing to decide. What good are all those olives out there if we do not extract the oil?"

"Yet knowing this, you shut the door a year ago and did not check the machinery again until the day you planned to use it."

"I meant to. Other things kept getting in the way."

Yosef removed a scraper from his toolbox and climbed into the circular granite pit where a pair of heavy wheels crushed the olives. Crossing to the central pivot, he poked around in the rancid residue of the prior year's pressings.

He freed a large glob of the smelly stuff and flicked it in

Anak's direction. "Do you mention to people how filthy your equipment is when they come to purchase oil for their table?"

"I did not ask you here to criticize my housekeeping. Regardless of what I should or should not have done, there are a few things you need to understand. First of all, the production of olive trees is cyclic. One year they yield less and the following year they yield bountifully. This is a bountiful year and I have already sent harvesters into the groves to work the trees."

He pointed to a covered receiving area. "Bags of olives will begin piling up out there within the hour. Olives *must be processed* for their oil as soon as possible after they are picked. If left to sit in bags for even a few days, they can mold and yield poor quality oil."

Stepping closer, Anak lowered his voice. "You must help me, Yosef. I have no one else I can turn to. Those are my uncle's trees out there. If he comes to check on things and finds nothing but lamp oil in a bountiful year, he will surely find someone else to run his business."

He clasped Yosef's hand. "I beg you, help me now and you will never want for olive oil as long as you live."

"If I am to do the work, it will be done my way," Yosef said.

Anak eagerly nodded. 'Whatever you say; you are in charge."

"Then we are going to rebuild the whole thing." Yosef called for a ladder. Climbing it to the ceiling, he disconnected the axis that supported the grinding wheels at the center of the pit. He measured it along with the wheel's axle and rotor. Next he estimated the length of the donkey-powered turning arm that Anak splintered. After recording the size and lengths of their replacements, he junked it all and sent two of the workmen to Dathan, the woodsman, with an urgent order for materials.

"While we wait," Yosef said as laborers carried out the broken pieces, "I want the pit and grinding wheels cleaned."

"This is not about housekeeping," Anak protested. "They turn, and that is all that matters."

Yosef stared him in the eye.

Anak quickly put men to work on the pit.

"How do the olives get to the crusher?" Yosef asked.

"The bags are stacked on the porch." Anak rolled aside a door and pointed to a bricked area with troughs and empty vats. "They are cleaned first. Once the leaves and sticks are removed, the olives are washed before they go into the crusher."

"And after that?"

Anak pointed to a doorway that led to an adjoining room. "When they have been reduced to a paste, it is shoveled into barrels. We add hot water and stir until the oil begins to separate out. When they are ready, the slurry is placed in fine mesh bags for crushing."

To his friend's dismay, Yosef insisted on inspecting the oil press.

Its huge fulcrum dominated the room. One end disappeared into the framework above a large holding tank. The opposite end, which ran to the other side of the room, had several chains supporting it. They'd suspended a pair of huge boulders from the fulcrum. Adjusting the chains allowed the operator to apply increasingly heavier loads to the bags of pulp to press out the oil.

Anak sighed with relief after Yosef inspected the apparatus and gave it his seal of approval.

The tour ended when the men returned from the wood yard. With materials in hand Yosef set about rebuilding the entire olive press piece by piece. Anak temporarily postponed the harvest while Yosef toiled through the night. By the next morning he'd finished refurbishing the press.

Anak's uncle showed up unannounced just as they finished filling the pit with olives for a test run. His eyes moved up and down noting all the new wood. "What have you done here? When did I approve this?"

Anak cleared his throat. "I, uh, noticed that the crusher was in need of repair. Knowing this will be a bountiful year, and not wanting to delay the harvest unnecessarily or bother you with minor details, I went ahead on my own. I hired Yosef, our local carpenter, to repair it. As you can see, he did a most excellent job."

His uncle put aside his misgivings after he inspected the work Yosef had done.

"One other thing, Uncle." Anak took his hand and tugged him over to the pit. "Notice how we changed the angle on the crushing wheels," he said, pointing. "They will operate more efficiently than before."

Locking eyes with Yosef, Anak gave him a quick, almost imperceptible nod. "As I was saying, while Yosef did his work *I redesigned* the way in which the crushing rollers attach to the pivot. If you allow me to order additional crushing wheels from the stonemason, Yosef can easily install them for this year's harvest. Having four mashing wheels instead of two reduces the crushing time thereby increasing our productivity." Anak grinned. "After all, this will be a bountiful year."

Anak waved everyone back against the walls. Taking the mule's lead rope, he led the animal in a circle, demonstrating how well the unit functioned with *his* modifications.

~ 8 ~

"The carpenter stretches a line, he marks it out with a pencil; he fashions it with planes, and marks it with a compass." ~ Isaiah 44:13

Miryam's mood greatly improved over the next few days. Rather than bother to knock, she simply opened the door and walked into Yosef's shop. As expected, he was at his workbench, head down and hard at work.

"Hello, it is me again," she said when he looked up. "Have you grown tired of my interruptions yet?"

He dusted his hands and straightened his tunic. "What a silly question. Your visits are a wonderful respite, not an interruption. How did it go with your mother?"

"Good, much better than I expected. I lit the incense first just as you suggested. Perhaps it made the difference. Hearing that you could repair the box satisfied Imma. After seeing the fine milking stool you made, she has confidence in your skills." Miryam thought for an instant before quickly adding, "I do too, of course."

"Did you come by to see how far along I am?"

"I come bearing gifts. For the next several days you shall feast on Imma's cooking." She pointed into her basket as she itemized the things she'd brought. "I have a crock of cucumbers preserved in vinegar, smoked fish cured with her special spices, and flaxseed crackers. I soaked the chickpeas all night and crushed them myself to make the hummus to go with your crackers. Imma also sent spelt cakes with cheese and honey along with dates stuffed with chopped almonds."

She glanced over at him and returned his smile.

"You can return the basket another time," Miryam said as she sat it aside. "But, as long as I am here, how *are* you coming with the repairs?"

"I was just about to start working on the box. I hoped to have it ready sooner, but I spent a day and a night making emergency repairs on an oil press. I also promised one of the drovers I would have a new yoke for him, so I had to complete it first."

"May I keep you company while you work?"

"You are more than welcome to stay. Though I do not know how interesting it will be watching me work."

"I find the things you do fascinating." She watched him lay out the pieces on the bench and gave him an expectant look. "What comes next?"

"Yesterday I marked off the sides on the board and cut it to size.

Now I must put in the groove that will hold the sides."

"Is it hard to do?"

"Not particularly. I have the old crone to help me,"

"Who?"

"Best if I show you." He reached under the workbench and extracted a wooden tool. It consisted of a central frame along with an adjustable gauge held in place by two thumb screws. The gauge moved from left to right, enabling the user to determine its line of cut. He held it up for her to examine. "I call it the old crone." He pointed to a narrow blade protruding from the bottom. "A single tooth, you see."

Miryam snickered.

"A smoothing plane cuts a strip nearly as wide as the tool itself." He rested his hand on what he'd called *the old crone*. "This is known as a plough plane. Rather than smoothing, it cuts a narrow groove down the board."

He ran a finger across the tabletop, etching a line through the sawdust. "Think of a farmer and his oxen. He ploughs the field, leaving a furrow in his wake." He shook his head and frowned. "There I go again. You probably find all this talk of carpentry boring."

"I enjoy listening to you. Would it not be easier to just make the bottom piece smaller so it fits in-between the sides?"

He flipped the box on its side for her to see. "That is how the box was originally made. And it is also why it flew apart when it struck the floor. Doing it this way provides more gluing surface when I re-assemble the parts."

He reached under the workbench and brought out a package wrapped in soft leather. Untying it, he removed a pair of brass calipers. "First, I must measure the width of the sides to see how big a groove I require."

He carefully measured and selected a blade of the proper width. He laid it on top of the side, rechecking before he inserted it into the plane. "If the groove is either too wide or too narrow, the sides will not fit flush with the outside edge." Yosef made the first pass. A thin curl of algumwood seemed to run ahead of the blade as it slid along.

He pulled the thin slip of wood out and set it aside. "More incense," he said with a sly wink and made another pass across the board.

In a short time Yosef had incised a recess on all four edges of the board. He took the side pieces, tested the fit and nodded with satisfaction.

"Is it time to put it back together?" Miryam asked.

"I want to clean all of the pieces first. Then I will re-glue them." He crossed the room and took down a small corked flask from high on the shelf.

Miryam watched with interest as he wrapped a piece of cloth around a stick. After dipping it into the flask, Yosef began dabbing at the seams of the joints. Once the liquid had saturated the joints, he set them aside to let it do its work.

"Why did you put water in the seams?"

"It is not water." He handed her the still damp cloth, allowing her to examine it.

While it had no identifiable odor, it exuded a strange volatility. "What is it called?" she asked, blinking her eyes.

"If it has a name, I do not know it." Sensing her confusion, he explained. "The Egyptians developed a way of using bronze tubes to capture the steam rising off of a pot of boiling wine. The resulting liquid is extremely flammable. They use it to produce sudden bursts of fire during their pagan rites and ceremonies. I call the process *capturing the spirit of the* wine. The Psalms speak of wine gladdening the heart of man. I believe it is this steam that does it."

Returning to the pieces on his workbench, Yosef wrapped the rag around his stick again and swabbed the boards, removing any lingering traces of old glue.

He gathered the pieces and set them aside. "That is all I can do for now. We must allow them to air out over night. In the morning I can re-assemble the box. I plan to use bull glue, the strongest there is, and clamp it while it dries." He smiled. "Then I will polish the box and deliver it to your door as promised."

Rounding his workbench, Yosef thanked her again for the treats and escorted her to the door. Pulling a curtain aside, he silently watched her cross the square. As always, his gaze followed her until she turned the corner and disappeared from view.

His life hadn't been the same since the first time Miryam came into his shop. A smile swept across his lips as he relived the events of that fateful afternoon. Something unique and unexplainable happened the moment she popped her head around the edge of the door.

He now realized she'd lived in his soul for as long as he could remember. Meeting her in the flesh for the first time was the fulfillment of a long held dream. In the depths of his heart he knew his life would never be complete without Miryam in it.

~ 9 ~

Yosef ended his workday early, washed, and put on a fresh tunic. He gave Anna's box a final inspection then wrapped it in a soft piece of hide.

Brimming with anticipation, he tucked the package under his arm and left for Yoachim's house. He crossed the village square and walked to the other side of town. He was about to fulfill the promise he'd made to Miryam two days earlier.

Anna smiled when she opened the door. "*Shalom Aleichem*, Yosef. it is good to see you. Come in, come in."

"*Aleichem Shalom*," Yosef said as he entered their home, "it is good to see you as well, Anna."

Her eyes went to the package under his arm. "I see you have brought my algum wood box back to me. Bless you, bless you." She shepherded him into the house and led him to a table in the front room.

He heard chopping sounds coming from the kitchen as they crossed the room. A pan clanked and a skillet sizzled.

Anna stood with her back to the kitchen, nervously fluttering her hands as she waited. "You must excuse me. I am beside myself with anticipation. I have looked forward to this moment ever since Miryam told me you could repair my treasured heirloom." She grinned. "And now, at last, the time has come for me to see your handiwork."

Miryam's smiling face suddenly appreaed around the corner. She gave Yosef a quick wave before disappearing back into the kitchen.

He placed the package in the center of the table with exaggerated care. He took hold of the string securing the piece of hide and tugged. When the knot opened and the wrapping fell away, he took a step back to await Anna's reaction.

She took one look and began blotting tears as she reached for it. Bringing it close, she slowly scrutinized each side. She removed the lid and turned the box over, studying his repair. After a long and thorough examination, she put it down and beamed up at him. "Better is the end of waiting than the beginning." She opened her arms wide. "Come, let me hug you. You have given me back what I thought was forever lost."

She caught Yosef's hand when he turned to leave. "Do not leave. You must stay and have supper with us. It is the least I can do." She cupped a hand around his ear. Leaning close, she whispered, "Miryam has worked all afternoon getting it ready for you." She raised a finger as a warning. "Do not let her know I gave away her secret."

Miryam rose and started stacking the plates and bowls after the meal.

Her mother stopped her. "You have done enough work for one day. Let the dishes go. I am sure our busy carpenter here has also put in a full day. You and Yosef should enjoy the cool of the evening by yourselves in the garden. Meanwhile, your father and I will take care of things in here," Anna said, shooing them out the door.

They crossed the stone patio side-by-side and slowly circled the yard. Miryam pointed out the various plantings as they walked.

"Unlike mine, your garden appears to be thriving, no doubt because of the tender care it receives. My little patch, on the other hand, barely keeps me alive," Yosef said with a self-deprecating chuckle.

Miryam arched an eyebrow. "Perhaps you would show more interest if you tended a forest instead of beans, peas and onions."

"In spite of what you imagine, I have not yet learned to eat wood," he said, pretending her comment had offended him.

"My spices and herbs are over here. Come take a look." She

grabbed his hand and tugged him along.

His fingers gently closed around hers as they walked. He continued holding her hand until she stooped to pinch off some wayward runners on the mint plants. She stacked them into a neat pile beside the walkway. Promising herself she'd come back and get them before they rooted, she rose brushing crumbs of dirt from her fingers.

Yosef shot a quick backward glance over his shoulder. Certain he would not be overheard, he lowered his voice and. took her hand. He gazed into her eyes. "Miryam, there is a matter of great importance that I wish to discuss with you."

His raised hand stifled any comment.

He took a deep breath. "I, of course, understand that tradition demands a man speak to a young woman's father if he desires to take her as his wife. However, you are of sufficient age to reject an offer of marriage. So I am coming to you first. I need to know if this is what you want." He stared at his feet and mumbled, "If you prefer I not say anything to him, I will understand. After all, you are a very pretty young woman who must have many suitors and I am merely a humble woodworker."

She threw her arms around his neck and rose onto her tiptoes to kiss him. "You silly man, of course it is what I want. Carpentry is interesting, but I come by your shop so often because it is you I want to see."

He embraced her and kissed her again. They continued to hold hands after separating, neither of them knowing quite what to say or do next.

"Well, I suppose everything is settled then," Yosef said, once he found his voice. "Now I must speak to your father about the matter."

"Yes," Miryam stammered, "my father. Yoachim, I mean Abba. He, um, he is in the house...that is where he lives."

Leaving the gardens, they strolled back toward the house

without another word. Anna heard their footsteps as they crossed the patio and came out to meet them. Leaving Yosef, Miryam raced ahead and grabbed her mother's arm. She pulled her aside and whispered in her ear.

Anna took her daughter by the hand and led her back across the patio to where Yosef waited. "Miryam and I are going to sit on the bench here in the garden for a few moments. Her father is inside, if you have anything you wish to discuss with him," she said with a sly wink.

~ 10 ~

"The foundations of Magdala, Arbel, Nazareth, and Jotapata appear for the first time in the Hasmonean period...the Jewish migration from Judea to Lower Galilee occurred sometime before 100 B.C." ~ J. H. Charlesworth & M. Aviam, *Reconstructing First-Century Galilee*

Yoachim was examining the box when Yosef entered the house. At the sound of footsteps, he raised his eyes and motioned his visitor closer.

Lifting the lid, the gray-haired man passed the box back and forth in front of his face and inhaled deeply. "It smells just the way it did when we were young. It is strange how our minds work. I had forgotten all about the wood's pleasant aroma, yet lifting the lid erases the years and takes me back to the moment Anna first showed it to me.

"You have done a fine job with the box. You cannot imagine how pleased my Anna was to have it back again." He ran a fingertip along the bottom edge. "You changed the way it was constructed. The bottom now extends out to the sides, making it visible."

"Yes, Perhaps I should not have changed its design without first consulting your wife. I did it to make the box stronger. I also cleaned and re-glued all of the joints. It should last her for many, many years."

"That presumes *we* will last many, many years," Yoachim said and laughed.

Miryam's father often traveled in his work. And even when he was at home, he and Yosef had not interacted much. Both of them found it difficult to span the gap in their ages and interests. Consequently their conversations, if one could call them that, had consisted of little more than polite snippets and terse replies tossed back and forth with minimal interest on either side.

It took only seconds for Yosef to realize that this night would be different, very different. While such trivial niceties greased the wheels of societal transactions, an interchange centered on one's health and the weather would not result in a betrothal.

Instead of the tired, somewhat distracted patriarch of the family, Yoachim seemed a font of energy this evening. He grinned and sat the box aside. "But you are not here to listen to an old man reminisce or talk about carpentry and gluing joints, are you? I sense there is something else on your mind, hmm?" He waved him into a chair. "Sit down and we will talk a bit, man to man."

Yosef smoothed his cloak and sat erect in the chair. "As you have surmised, I came to ask for your daughter's hand in marriage. I know I have only been here in Nazareth for a relatively short time, but anyone who has done business with me will vouch for my honesty. I am a just man, a devout Jew who adheres to the Law and the Prophets."

Yoachim leaned back and smoothed his beard as he listened. "What about the admonition given to Moses that the people of Israel shall marry within the family of the tribe of their father?"

Yosef interpreted his indefinite response as a demand for further proof. "I am of the tribe of Yudah, descended from the Royal Line of David through his son and heir, Solomon the Wise." He gave him a nervous smile, "Although I am clearly not a king, or even a prince. I am but a simple carpenter as was my father, Ya'akov, and my grandfather, Matthan, before him."

Yoachim's eyes briefly settled on the algum wood box then returned to the eager young man sitting across from him. "The Lord loves the humble man, but do not understate your abilities by calling yourself a *simple carpenter*. You are a skilled craftsman, a true artisan."

Yosef dipped his head, acknowledging the compliment. When Yoachim said no more, Yosef soldiered on.

"I am a hard worker, and have always been able to find work." He leaned forward, earnestly pressing his case. "I do not aspire to riches. I desire a good wife more than great wealth. I will be a faithful husband to Miryam. I give you my oath here and now that neither your daughter nor her children shall ever lack the necessities of life."

Yoachim folded his hands across his stomach, interlacing his fingers. "Earlier you spoke of your father in the past tense."

"Yes. Sadly, he and my mother now rest in Abraham's bosom."

"I am sorry to hear of your loss. Do you have any family?"

"My older brother, Tovit, took over my father's business after Abba died. He still lives in Bethlehem with his wife and children. My sisters have all married and have children. Some live in Bethlehem, one in Jerusalem, another in Jaffa. I also have many cousins here in the Galilee. Several branches of my family relocated during the Great Migration which occurred under the reign of the Hasmonean King, Alexander Jannaeus."

Yoachim nodded with understanding. "It seems many of us Galileans are transplanted Judeans. My family and Anna's also came here at that time. Why? Because Alexander Jannaeus needed loyal Jews to secure the land as he expanded the borders of his kingdom. And come they did. Free land is a powerful incentive. Do you know any of your relatives here in the Galilee?"

"I know one or two. The others are merely names in a list, people I have never met." Yosef shrugged. "After all, the Great Migration occurred over three generations ago. Time and distance have weakened those familial ties."

"Another connection we share. We have lost track of most of our family in the south. However, Anna does remain close to a cousin in Beth HaKerem. We sometimes visit Elisheva when we go to Jerusalem for the pilgrim Festivals. Her husband, Zecharias, is a priest at the Temple."

Yoachim folded his arms across his chest and stared at Yosef straight on. "An offer of marriage is a weighty matter, certainly not something to be done without forethought. Since you have no family close at hand, who have you discussed this with?"

"I have sought the counsel of the Lord in daily prayer. You see, Miryam carved an indelible mark on my heart the first day she came into my shop. For some time now I have loved her with a silent, patient and respectful love. Always maintaining an appropriate distance between us, of course."

"How will your family in Judea feel about you marrying a Galilean woman?"

"They accepted that possibility when I left home to come here." The ring in Yosef's fingers sparkled in the lamplight when he held it out to Yoachim. "With your permission, I would like to offer this ring to your daughter Miryam tonight."

Yoachim's weathered face crinkled into familiar smile lines. They rose together. The older man clasped Yosef's hand then hugged him. "Welcome to our family, my son. Since the day Miryam returned with the stool, she has spoken of nothing but you. Each night I receive the latest news about *Yosef the carpenter* as I eat my evening meal." He laughed. "Anna and I have been anticipating your visit."

"Come, let us share some wine then we will tell the women," Yoachim said as he crossed the room. He removed an amphora from a cabinet and carried it to the table along with two glasses and a cruet of water.

"May I," Yosef asked, resting a hand on the amphora of Galilean wine.

Yoachim replied with the flick of the hand.

"Besides being of the same tribe, your family and mine share a common history." Yosef sat their glasses side-by side. Then, instead of filling them with wine and diluting it with water as they normally did, he poured the wine directly into the cruet instead. "Let one of the glasses represent Judea and the other Galilee. I pour the same drink into them both. Neither contains pure wine nor pure water. What is in Judea is also in Galilee, and what is in Galilee is also in Judea."

Yosef lifted his glass, toasting his future father-in-law. "I raise my glass in memory of those who have gone before us, your ancestors and mine, to those we left behind and those who now stand beside us."

"And, as children of Avraham, to the common blood that flows within our veins," Yoachim added before taking a sip of wine.

~ 11 ~

"In the sixth month the angel Gabriel was sent from God to a city of Galilee named Nazareth, to a virgin betrothed to a man whose name was Joseph, of the house of David..."

~ Luke 1:26-27

Yoachim rested his arm around Yosef's shoulder as they walked to the yard where the women waited. Leaning close, he confided, "It is good to have this matter settled. Anna and I are not young any more, and Miryam is all we have. Her welfare and happiness are my primary concern. Knowing she will have someone like you to care for her when we pass on lifts a great burden from my mind."

Anna glanced up and smiled when she noticed her husband's arm over Yosef's shoulder. Miryam, less confident of the outcome, sat quietly beside her mother with hands folded in her lap as she nervously awaited her father's decision.

"Anna, this brash young man seems to think repairing a family heirloom somehow gives him the right to come into our home and make demands," Yoachim said. "He has asked...no, he insisted, that I allow him to take our beloved Miryam as his wife. Have you ever heard of such a thing?"

"True, he is brash. He also appears somewhat dangerous. It seems he has left no choice in the matter. If you do not agree, who knows what he will do? He might even threaten our lives," Anna said, stifling a grin.

"I do hope this is what Miryam wants." Yoachim said with a mischievous twinkle in his eye.

Miryam leaped off of the bench and ran to hug her father. "You know it is what I want, Abba." She kissed his cheek then stepped beside Yosef. When he reached for her hand, she shyly slipped her fingers into his.

The following *Shabbat* Yosef and Miryam and their

witnesses, along with family, friends, and neighbors gathered in the synagogue to sanctify the betrothal.

After completing the day's Torah readings, the Rabbi asked the couple and their witnesses to join him on the *bimah*. Yosef rose first. He wore his best cloak and his hair and beard were neatly trimmed. He led the way with Anak trailing behind him. Since Miryam had traveled to Capernaum to serve as witness when Zebedee and her kinswoman, Salome, were betrothed, they returned the favor by coming to Nazareth so Salome could be Miryam's witness.

Miryam was dressed in white. Salome had oiled her hair and tied it with ribbons. They left the women's section and joined the men on the raised platform at the front of the building.

The rabbi positioned Yosef and Miryam in the center behind a small table with their witnesses on either side. Smoothing his gray beard, he took his place behind the podium.

Moving his eyes over those assembled there, he said, "Let it be known that on this, the eighth day of the month of *Sh'vat* in the year 3,755 of the World, in this community in Nazareth of Galilee; before truthful and sober witnesses, and before this holy congregation: come these, the bride, Miryam, daughter of Yoachim, and the bridegroom, Yosef, son of Ya'akov, to unite and bond together, joining one to the other in a Covenant of Love, to thus make a household amongst the People of Israel."

He paused long enough to give the couple a reassuring smile then continued. "This partnership which Miryam and Yosef effect, shall be a sacred covenant, like those ancient covenants which our forefathers set in olden days; like the great covenant that the Blessed Creator made with our father, Avraham, and thus changed the fate of the world.

"This is a covenant of faith and hope, like the covenant that the Blessed Creator swore to Noah and his descendants, as it is said: 'When I bring clouds over the earth and the bow is seen in the clouds, I will remember my covenant which is between me and you and every living creature of all flesh; and the waters shall never again become a flood to destroy all flesh."

The Rabbi left the podium carrying an amphora of wine. He approached the table in front of them and uncorked it. He filled one of the cups nearly to the top, carefully blotted the amphora's spout on a cloth, and filled the other half full.

"You see two cups before you," he said, passing his hand over them. "By your choice, only one of the cups is reserved for the two of you alone. You will share the first cup with those who have been partners in your lives thus far, the ones who have helped to make you the individuals you are."

He raised the cup, blessing it. "This cup of wine symbolizes the gratitude Miryam and Yosef have for the loving care and teaching of parents, the ties of heart and mind and memory that link brothers and sisters, and for the friendships that fill this cup to overflowing."

Yosef took it from him and offered it to Anak. After Anak took a tiny sip, Yosef handed it to Miryam. She offered the wine to Salome. Leaving their witnesses on the platform, Miryam and Yosef took the cup to her parents. After her parents sipped from the cup, they moved among the congregation offering it to all the others.

When they returned with the empty cup, the Rabbi blessed the other one, saying, "Blessed art thou, *Adoni*, Ruler of the universe, Creator of the fruit of the vine. You have also sanctified us with your commandments and commanded us concerning illicit relations. This cup of wine is symbolic of the cup of life. As you share this cup of wine, you undertake to share all the future may bring. May you find life's joys doubly gladdened, its bitterness sweetened, and all things hallowed by true companionship and love."

Yosef and Miryam took the cup from the Rabbi and recited together, "Just as the laws of Moses and Israel are of Divine origin and bear the seal of truth, so shall our marriage be consecrated. And, as the laws of Moses and Israel forever consecrate all those who enter into its covenant, so shall we be consecrated forever."

Flushed with nervousness, Miryam sipped a little of the wine then handed the cup to Yosef. He carefully brought it to his lips and finished it. He sat the empty cup aside and took her hand. After slipping a golden band onto her finger, he stared into her eyes. "Miryam, daughter of Yoachim, behold you are sanctified to me, behold you are betrothed to me, behold you are my wife."

The Rabbi blessed them saying, "May the Lord bless and keep you. May the Lord cause his countenance to shine upon you and be gracious unto you. May the Lord favor you and grant you peace."

Salome hugged Miryam and Anak patted Yosef on the back. The entire assembly gathered around them, shepherding the couple back to Yoachim and Anna's house where a feast awaited them.

~ 12 ~

"Three times in the year you shall keep a feast to me. You shall keep the feast of unleavened bread; as I commanded you, you shall eat unleavened bread for seven days at the appointed time..." ~ Exodus 23:14-15

Making a public commitment to each other added an undertone of urgency to Yosef and Miryam's lives. True, Jewish tradition favored long betrothals, meaning the day of their wedding still lay far into the future. It would be at least a year before she became Yosef's lawfully wedded spouse and he took her into his home and bed.

In the meantime, they both had work, much work, to do. Between them they had a single year to accumulate all the everyday essentials of life. Like most young women in the village, Miryam had a trunk in the corner of her room designated for her trousseau. Also like most young women of the village, filling it with the paraphernalia of daily life never seemed a particularly urgent task. Everything changed when a certain carpenter appeared on the scene and asked to take her as his bride.

For his part, Yosef was a step ahead of most potential bridegrooms. He already owned a house and had enough utensils to survive as a bachelor. Still, the prospect of bringing Miryam into his home in its current state distressed him. He created a long list of essential tasks he needed to complete before the wedding. Among the items on this list was additional work on the roof, constructing new cabinets for her kitchen, and building several pieces of furniture.

Now that their relationship was out in the open and formalized, they were free to spend more time together. Miryam began dropping by his shop each afternoon on the days Yosef worked in Nazareth. Since he made it a practice to walk her home, Anna routinely set an extra place for him at their supper table.

Miryam put her sewing aside and glanced across the room. "Do you plan on journeying to Jerusalem for the Feast of Unleavened Bread?"

Yosef lifted his eyes from his workbench with a puzzled look. "Of course I will be going for the Pesach. How could you even imagine I would not?"

"Must you always be so serious?" She laughed and gave him a peck on the cheek. "It was only my way of inviting you to accompany us. Abba wanted me to ask."

Rising to his full height, Yosef thrust his shoulders back and brushed aside a curl of wood clinging to his forearm. "You are now my betrothed wife; it is my duty to escort you to Jerusalem."

As the time of the Festival drew near, processions of pilgrims formed in each of the villages. While a number of roads furnished access to Jerusalem, the preferred route from Nazareth originated in Capernaum. It left the shores of Lake Gennesareth at Magdala. Turning to the southwest, it followed the curving foothills of Mt. Tabor then passed through the village of Nain. It headed east after leaving Nain and circled Mt. Moreh near where the invading Midianites had encamped centuries earlier. The route met the ancient Jordan Valley trade route at Seythopolis. Heading due south, the throng followed the Jordan River to Jericho, turned and went to Jerusalem.

Yoachim's little family group mingled with Jewish families from other cities in the Galilee. These regular pilgrimages provided a chance to renew old friendships and catch up on the latest family news. Each time Yoachim spotted an old friend or acquaintance, he clutched Yosef's arm and drug him over to meet them. The old man's chest puffed out and his eyes sparkled as he proudly said, "I want you to meet *my son*."

For her part, Anna said little about Miryam's betrothal to the people they met. Instead, her thoughts focused on the melancholy prospect of losing her daughter. Seeing Miryam happily walking beside Yosef filled her with nostalgia and a longing for times past.

At the end of each day the convoys gathered around fires to eat and rest. While Yoachim joked and swapped stories with the men, his wife sat in the dark watching the flickering flames play off her daughter's face. Anna noticed her smile as she and Yosef conversed in low tones. When Miryam laughed and rested her head on Yosef's shoulder, his arm encircled her.

Anna remembered holding her close as an infant, caressing her and doting on her. A swirl of emotions urged Anna to grab her and hold her close once again. But she couldn't. Though she would always be her daughter, Miryam was no longer hers to hold. She belonged to another now. Like it or not, her time had come and gone. The future belonged to them.

For as long as Miryam could remember, they had always celebrated the Passover in the home of Yoachim's boyhood friend, Shachar. This year would be no different.

Shachar lived in the oldest section of Jerusalem, an area known as the *City of David*. Unlike the rest of the city, the neighborhood had its own walls, a remnant of an earlier era. The district sat on a wide ridge with the Tyropoean Valley on one side and the Kidron Valley on the other. This roughly triangular area began at the ancient gate to the Spring of Gihon and terminated at the south wall of Herod's Temple.

"Having more people again this year is not a cause for worry." Yoachim slapped his old friend on the back and grinned. "So our families keep growing, this is a good thing. With Miryam now betrothed, I am already looking forward to my first grandchild."

Shachar eased a drape aside and pointed at the lamb grazing in his back yard. "I purchased the biggest lamb I could find. Do you think there will be enough for everyone?"

"We always have just the right amount. Any excess can go to those we invite in off the street. After all, when have the poor ever complained if someone slips a few extra slices of meat onto their plates?"

The two men left the front room and walked into the large dining room. Yosef rose when they entered and put aside his tools. "I have completed the extension for your table," he said. "I was just cleaning up."

Yosef led Shachar over so he could examine the work. "As you requested, I built them as large as possible."

Shachar gave a low whistle as he ran his eyes from one end of the table to the other. "Any longer and we could not enter the room."

Yosef directed his attention to the place where the two pieces merged with the table. "The extensions are joined to the underside for stability. It will be easy to separate them after the feast and store them for future use." Yosef stooped to straighten the corner of a rug he'd folded back, and left.

"They do not look sturdy enough," Shachar whispered once Yosef was out of earshot. "What if the whole thing crashes down right in the middle of our Seder meal taking the women and children with it? Everyone from one end of Jerusalem to the other will hear of it. I could become a laughingstock."

"It *will not* collapse. My son, Yosef, is the best carpenter in the Galilee. Those extensions he built are probably the strongest piece of furniture in this house."

"Look at them. They are bare wood. They have no finish, no polish." Shachar frowned as he ran his hand over the bare planks set atop the hastily built stands. "Is this any way to celebrate the *Pesach*?"

"They are meant for one night only," Yoachim said, trying to calm him. "No one will see what lies beneath the tablecloth." He winked. "Everyone will be concentrating on the marvelous treats the women have prepared for us."

Yoachim and Shachar took a stairway to the roof so they could study the Festival crowds.

"Rich or poor, every year they come," Shachar said. He swept an arm toward the orderly rows of black goat hair tents marching up the Mount of Olives like an army of ants.

The Torah commanded that the children of Israel must consume the Passover lamb within the walls of Jerusalem. And so, like an immense flock of homing pigeons, Jews throughout the Empire returned for the *Pesach*. Each year's Festival brought with it an overwhelming sense of joy which permeated every street, courtyard, and home. Neither the city's residents nor the visitors minded the tent cities that sprang up on the hills surrounding the Holy City.

From the rooftop the men watched a continuous river of travelers pouring through the city gates. Like Yoachim and his family, many stayed with friends or relatives. Those without such connections filled the streets waiting for someone to invite them in to share the Seder meal.

~ 13 ~

"This took place towards the end of the winter, and many of the clay ovens had already been set in their places in anticipation of the upcoming festival." ~ Mishna, Tractate Ta'anit 3:8

While the men waited for the designated time to take the lamb to the Temple and loaded fuel into the roasting ovens, back at the house the woman and children busied themselves with final preparations.

Older boys clustered in the backyard carefully filling lamps with oil. Special linens came out of closets as the tables were set. In the kitchen women chopped, diced and sliced, while others stirred steaming pots on the stove. Another group clustered around a central table assembling a variety of desserts.

With the preparations well in hand, everyone took a much needed rest before regrouping for the serious work of serving the evening's meal began in earnest.

Miryam was walking down a hallway and noticed a young girl sitting in the yard beside Shachar's Paschal lamb. She watched her pluck tufts of fresh grass from the lawn and feed them to the lamb. Deciding to visit with Shoshana, she exited the house walking in her direction.

Although she only saw her during the Festivals, Miryam knew her story well. This lovely girl child, the fulfillment of her parent's dreams, failed to thrive as an infant. An affectionate child, and loved by all who knew her, Shoshana was slow to walk, talk and master other social skills. Her rounder, flatter face with small nose and upward slanting eyes marked her as one of those who would always require a bit of help in life.

Sitting on the bench beside her, Miryam wished her a happy Passover festival. *"Pesach Sameach,* Shoshana. How are you today?"

The girl didn't respond. When she took a closer look, Miryam noticed tears dribbling down the girl's cheeks. "Is something wrong?"

Shoshana sniffed and ground her fists into her eyes. "Imma told me I have to ask the questions this year. She said it is past time and I must do it."

"Congratulations, that is a very great honor. I am sure you will make your parents very proud."

Shoshana's bottom lip puffed out. "I will not."

"Whatever makes you say such a thing?"

"Every time I try, I get all mixed up and cannot say the words in the right order. When it comes time for me to sing, I will do a bad job and everyone will hate me."

Miryam couldn't help but laugh. She put her arms around the sad girl and hugged her. "No one could ever hate you, Shoshana." She pointed across the yard to a spot hidden from view. "Let's go over there where no one will see us and you can try singing it for me."

"How old are you?" Miryam asked as they crossed the yard.

Shoshana tucked in her thumbs and extended the fingers on both hands. She was eight years old. Most children could sing the *Mah Nishtanah,* or *the four questions,* by age four with minimal coaching.

"Give it a try so I can see how you do."

Though she struggled mightily, completing the short chant eluded the little girl. Having amply demonstrated her inability to perform this simple task, she hung her head and mumbled, "I told you I could not do it."

"I have an idea." Miryam said. "What if we practiced together? I could sing it with you."

They practiced until Shoshana could mimic Miryam's words perfectly.

Miryam hugged her tightly. "See. I knew you could do it, and you did."

The girl's bright grin quickly faded as doubts crept back in. "I can do it *now*, but everyone will be watching tonight. I will become afraid and forget everything."

"I have an idea," Miryam said, and whispered in the girl's ear.

Shoshana's eyes widened. "Will we get in trouble?"

Miryam gave a conspiratorial wink. "The only way to find out is to try it. I think it is worth the risk, what about you?

Family, friends and guests gathered in the dining room as the sun set. Throughout the room people wished their tablemates *Pesach Sameach*. The room gradually darkened as night fell over the city. They had lighted the lamps by the time Shachar and Yoachim entered the room carrying the roasted lamb. They sat it on the sideboard and took their places at either end of the table.

Miryam took a seat beside her nervous little friend and complimented Shoshanna on the pretty ribbons in her hair.

Shoshanna didn't feel pretty; she felt like a prisoner being led to their execution. Raising her head, she gave the room a quick once-over. Everyone was in their place. Her palms grew damp with sweat. Everyone is ready, she thought, everyone but me.

Shoshana's heart raced when her grandfather rose. Shachar's happy face glowed in the lamplight. His eyes slowly moved around the table, pausing for a moment on each person. "*Pesach Sameach* to you all," he said. Scattered returns of *Pesach Sameach* echoed from around the table.

Shachar opened an amphora of wine, poured a little in his glass and passed to the person on his right. He waited until the amphora had passed from hand to hand, making a circuit around the room. Once everyone's glass held some wine, he said the *Havdalah*, the prayer of sanctification, over the wine. He raised his cup when he finished and everyone drank the first cup of wine together.

Servants brought in a basin and towels so everyone could wash their hands after the first glass of wine. Next, they took the leafy green on their Seder plate. Dipping it in a nearby dish of salted water, they gently shook off the excess and ate it. Shoshanna accidently shoved hers all the way into the dish. Flustered, she pulled the soppy leaf out and swung it back and forth, throwing water droplets on everyone around her.

Head down, she crammed the entire leaf into her mouth and chewed. Fear rose in her throat when she heard movement at the front of the table. She watched her grandfather remove a matzo and break it in two. A sense of expectancy filled the room. From across the table her mother gave Shoshana a little wink, indicating it was time to start the questions.

The little girl sat still as a statue.

A hush spread over the room as everyone watched her nervously lick her lips.

The tablecloth hid Miryam's arm. She reached over and clasped the girl's shaky hand.

Shoshana took a deep breath and sang out, *"Mah nishtanah, halailah hazeh, mikol haleilot?"* asking her grandfather, "Why is this night different from all the other nights?"

Under the table Shoshana clutched Miryam's hand with all her might, as one-by-one she flawlessly conversed with her grandfather in chant. That night she asked each of the four questions as required, helping to fulfill the Torah command to repeat the story of the Exodus each *Pesach*.

After the meal Shoshana spotted Miryam outside the dining room and ran to her. She threw her arms around her and hugged her. "Oh, thank you, thank you, thank you, Miryam. I could not have done it without you. It worked just like you said it would. No one even knew you were singing with me."

Miryam smiled. "That is because I was not singing."

Shoshana put her hands on her hips. "Yes you were. I heard your voice and I sang along just like in the yard this afternoon."

"It is kind of you to credit me for your success, but I did not sing with you."

"Why not? You said you would."

Miryam rested her arm on her shoulder. Leaning close, she tried to calm the girl's roiling emotions. "I said I would join you if you needed my help. I did not have to. You did fine all by yourself."

"But I heard singing." Fear and confusion widened the girl's eyes. "If you were not singing with me, who was it?"

"I believe it was your angel," Miryam said after a little thought. "The Psalms promise that God will give his angels charge over you to guard you in all your ways."

Shoshana's brow furrowed as she mulled over this information. "Do you think I really heard an angel?" she asked in a tone of incredulity.

Miryam nodded.

Shoshana tilted her head back and moved it in a slow circle, examining the ceiling. She tiptoed over to the door and checked behind it. Finding nothing, she glanced over at Miryam, lifted her eyebrows and shrugged.

~ 14 ~

"In those days Mary arose and went with haste into the hill country, to a city of Judah..." ~ Luke 1:39

The family left Jerusalem at the end of Pesach and retraced their way home. Life settled back into established routines. Miryam spent her days weaving cloth and sewing the items she'd need after the wedding. For his part, Yosef continued building his business in Sepphoris and began putting money aside to provide the security he wanted to have for his bride.

This period of normality lasted less than two weeks. Then, without warning, the patterns of their lives underwent a radical change.

Yosef had fallen into the habit of walking over to Miryam's house for an evening visit on the days when she didn't come to the shop. He tapped at the door, waited a moment, and then entered. Anna looked up and smiled as she watched him come into the house. "It is good to see you again, my son." She rose and opened her arms to him.

He kissed her cheek as they hugged. "Like always, it is a pleasure, Imma Anna."

She held him at arm's length and ran her eyes over him. "You look a little pale. Are you hungry? I can fix you something to eat."

He shook his head. "Do not trouble yourself over me. I already ate at home."

She gave him an indulgent frown as they crossed the room together. "You are family now. I will trouble myself over you, whether you like it or not. A man living by himself is at loose ends. You need a woman to look after you."

"Right you are, and I shall soon have one." He gave her a delighted grin. "And then Imma Anna will no longer have to worry about her Yosef."

She made shushing noises. "Show me the mother who stops worrying about her children just because they are grown." She gave him a friendly shove. "Be gone. I refuse to waste time debating with a fool. Miryam is working in the yard."

Miryam stopped her grinding and dusted her hands when she saw Yosef step out of the house. "It is good to see you, my husband," she said when he embraced her. "How was your day? Were you able to complete the plough Remi'el ordered?"

"I finished it and Remi'el came for it a short while ago." He shook his head. "Why are some people never satisfied? I produced the plough on time just as he asked using the best quality wood. My plough will last longer than Remi'el will, yet he still muttered about the cost. He knows as well as I that anyone else would have charged him more, not less."

She patted his hand. "It is as we have often observed, 'Some people are not happy unless they are unhappy.'" Miryam shifted on the bench, preparing to rise. "Have you had your evening meal? I could get something from the kitchen if you are hungry."

Yosef chuckled.

Her cheeks warmed. "Why do you laugh?"

"You need not get me anything. I ate before I came. My father always counseled me to carefully study a girl's mother before I asked for her hand in marriage. He said most young men fail to realize that to marry a young woman is in effect to marry her mother."

Miryam stared into her lap. "Are you now jesting about me or about Imma? When you are with the men, perhaps you and your friends snicker at us both."

He slide over beside her and took her hand. "I would never do such a thing. Your mother already offered to feed me. I find the resemblance between you and your mother pleasing...endearing." Yosef put a finger under Miryam's chin. Gently lifting her chin, he stared into her eyes. "Please do not be angry with me. I would never do anything to hurt you."

Her smile put the sparkle back in his eyes.

"My father also often said, 'He who has found a good wife has found something of great value, and will obtain favor with the Lord.'" He shook his head. "But I have not merely found a *good wife*. No, I have found the *best wife* a man could ever hope for. I so wish my parents could meet their beautiful new daughter."

"Like you, I wish your parents could be with us when we wed." Miryam bit her lip. She studied the paving stones beneath her feet as she searched for her next words. "Yosef, there is something I must tell you. I feel I should visit my Cousin Elisheva."

Hands clasped in her lap, Miryam listened to a bee buzzing among the flowers as she awaited his response.

"You want to visit Elisheva, the wife of Zecharias the priest, who lives in Judea near Jerusalem? Are your parents going as well?"

Miryam shook her head. "No, just me."

"Have you thought this through? We just returned from Jerusalem. Why did you not visit when we were so close?"

She struggled for her words. "I did not know then what I know now."

"What is so important that it necessitates a trip back to Judea?"

"She is with child and I must go to be with her."

"How can your cousin be with child? You told me Elisheva is barren and past her child-bearing years."

"With God all things are possible," she said, softly.

He scratched his head. "True enough, but how could you possibly know what is happening in Judea when you are here in Galilee?"

She avoided his intense stare. "A messenger told me. He, he uh, came this morning while I was alone in the house. No one spoke with him except me."

"And because of this messenger you feel you must go all the way to Judea?"

She took his rough hands in hers and pressed them to her lips. "I must, for many reasons. There is a caravan leaving for Jerusalem the day after the *Shabbat*. I made arrangements to travel with them."

His eyebrows shot up. "And you did all of this without speaking to me first?"

She gave a rueful nod. Her answer, when it came, was hardly more than a whisper. "It was not my intention to act without consulting you. But I feared I might not find passage if I delayed."

"Then you are not asking; you are telling." Yosef kneaded his temples and sighed deeply. "I cannot say this news pleases me, yet for some unknown reason you clearly feel strongly about it." He sighed. "If you must go, I will not stand in your way. May HaShem protect you."

Miryam swiveled on the bench and hugged him. "Thank you, Yosef. This means more to me than you can imagine."

"What did your father say when you told him?"

"I have not told him yet," she said with a guilty look. A moment later her countenance unexpectedly brightened. She gave him a peck on the cheek. "Since we are betrothed, I am no longer my father's daughter. I am now Yosef's betrothed wife. Hearing that you have agreed to me making the trip will set his mind at ease."

Early the next morning Yosef visited Dathan, the woodsman. Dathan's men went high into the Karmel Mountains cutting timber. After removing the branches and top they sawed the trees into manageable lengths. They used oxen to haul the logs back to his compound.

Once inside the warehouse, Yosef walked up and down the rows of boards with Dathan at his side. "Is this all the wood you have?" he asked after they'd inspected every stack.

"Are you never satisfied? Several months ago you came in here wanting algum wood. You are always careful when selecting your wood, but this is the first time you have not found a single piece that pleases you. Who commissioned this job, Herod the King...Caesar of Rome?"

"I am making a gift and I want the wood to be the very best it can be."

"Why did you not tell me this in the beginning? Wait here."

Dathan returned a few moments later with a broad smile and several boards tucked under his arm. "These you will like, my friend. I have been carefully drying this almond wood for a year. All the cut ends are sealed with wax." He slowly turned one of the boards in the sunlight. "You do not find quality like this every day. Look at the dense, even grain. Imagine how beautiful they will become when you are finished with them."

Yosef took a board from him. He quietly studied the grain on one side then flipped it over to scrutinize the back. He held it out at arm's length and cocked his head, checking it for warping or cupping. Sitting the board down, he spread his fingers and stepped them along its length. He put it aside and repeated the process with each of the others. A second board eventually joined the first.

"These two will be enough," Yosef said.

When it came time to pay, he attempted to haggle with the woodsman on the price, but he had already revealed far too much to make it a fruitful endeavor. In truth, he wanted the best and didn't much care what the boards cost. He paid Dathan and returned to his workshop, whistling as he walked.

~ 15 ~

Late in the afternoon, after he'd completed his other work, Yosef cooked up a stain from a mixture of tree bark, roots, and nut shells. He pushed the pot into the ashes from supper and scooped the remaining embers around it before he left to visit with friends. By the time he returned the warmth of the dying fire would have drawn out the pigments and concentrated the mixture, giving it the undertones and character he desired.

Hours later he hurried home in fading sunlight, eager to inspect his newest batch of stain. Yosef snatched a rag off of the table as he crossed the shadowy room. Wrapping the cloth around his hand just in case, he caught the pot's thick wire handle. He lifted it out of the fire pit and carried it into his workshop.

He lit a lamp and pulled up a stool before carefully straining his stew through a sieve. After he removed the plant material, he dipped the corner of a rag into the dark liquid and slathered it over a scrap piece of wood.

While the stain penetrated the grain of the wood, he poured the rest of it into a small amphora and cleaned the pot. Returning to the workbench, he wiped away the excess and held the scrap to the light. The wood had a rich deep brown cast. He slowly rotated it in his hand and smiled.

Miryam will love it, he thought, as he headed into the house to begin his evening prayers.

Early in the morning after the *Shabbat* Yosef answered a knock at his door and found Miryam dressed in a traveling cloak with a knapsack slung over her shoulder. "I wanted to say good-bye before I go. I am leaving for Beth HaKerem."

"So early?" He scratched and yawned then glanced out the window at the thin rim of sunlight breaking over the distant mountain peaks. "The sun is barely over the horizon."

"I am meeting the caravan at Sepphoris." She adjusted the strap of her knapsack, preparing to leave.

Yosef's work had kept him busy and they hadn't had much time to be together in the days since she first spoke of going to visit her kinswoman, Elisheva. He perceived an amazing change in Miryam in the few short days they'd been apart. Though he couldn't put his finger on it, the subtle difference was unmistakable. He sensed an indefinable power in the way Miryam moved and acted.

She was no longer the same young woman who had been driven to near panic over a damaged heirloom. Instead, she projected a sense of abiding peace. Though he couldn't explain it, Yosef definitely liked the way Miryam's face radiated this inner tranquility. Buoyed by this unseen confidence, the difficulties and hazards of traveling alone didn't seem to faze her.

"I have something for you to take with you," Yosef said over his shoulder as he headed for his workshop.

He emerged a few moments later with a broad smile and a package wrapped in hide. "I made something for Cousin Elisheva. Well, it is actually for her baby." Yosef laid the package on the table and loosed the bindings. Knowing she was restless to leave, he added, "It will only take a few moments for me to show it to you."

She'd worried after Yosef's less than enthusiastic reaction to the news of her trip to Beth HaKerem. The thought that she might have upset him had been uppermost in her mind these last few days. Yet in spite of any misgivings, he'd taken time to prepare a gift. Miryam found his actions endearing, reassuring.

The package contained five boards each stained a rich brown color and polished with beeswax and oil until they gleamed.

Miryam absentmindedly slid a fingertip over the top board. Its lustrous sheen and smooth surface fascinated her. "Your boards are beautiful. What are they for?"

"I made a cradle for her new baby." He grinned. "Let me show you how easy it is to assemble."

Yosef quickly sorted the parts across the tabletop. He pointed to a single board with rockers attached to it. "This is the bottom piece. It fits into the groove I cut into each of the sides." He flipped the bottom piece on end and aligned it between the two side pieces. The sides sloped when fit against the bottom, making the opening at the top wider than at the bottom. Both of the remaining pieces, the ends, tapered to match the angle of the sides. He'd cut two rectangular holes into each of them.

"Both of the sides have a pair of tenons at each end." He touched the extension. "I'll hold the sides while you fit their tenons through the mortices cut into the ends."

Miryam held one of the boards, rotating it slightly until the tenons aligned with the holes in the end piece. Only after she slipped it on did she notice that the portion of tenon extending out had a small slot cut in it.

"These pins secure the sides." Yosef picked up some tapered pegs and slid them into the slots, effectively locking the joint in place. He flipped the cradle over and they repeated the process. When they finished, he sat the cradle on its rockers and gently moved it back and forth. "There it is, ready for the new baby."

Miryam smiled. "How very clever you are. I am sure she will treasure it."

He slipped the pegs out and quickly disassembled the cradle. Re-wrapping them in the piece of hide, he tied it and gave the parcel a loving pat. "There it is, packed and ready for your trip."

"I do not know how to thank you. It must have taken a lot of time and effort."

"I am a carpenter; it is what I do."

Miryam nervously eyed the package on the table. "How heavy is it?"

He picked up the package and slipped it under his left arm.

"You need not worry about its weight. I will accompany you to Sepphoris." He held the door for her as they left. "I will give the leader of the caravan a little something to store it with his trade goods so you are not forced to carry it all the way to Beth HaKerem."

Miryam paused on the doorstep, waiting as he secured the door. She glanced back at him over her shoulder. They remained there, frozen in the moment, silently staring into each other's eyes. He read the affection in her upturned gaze and she felt the protective warmth in his.

"The caravan's route takes them very close to Beth HaKerem," she said as they crossed the village square. "It will be no trouble for me to carry the package to Cousin Elisheva's home."

Yosef nodded to the town's blacksmith as they left Nazareth. They followed a sloping path, weaving between terraced fields of fruit trees and vegetables. Several of their neighbors were already at work. They paused from their hoeing long enough to smile and wave to the young couple as they passed.

Their path took them alongside a walled vineyard with a winepress in the center. Yosef noticed an errant branch protruding over the rock wall and plucked off a small cluster of grapes. Miryam lowered her eyebrows, frowning in mock disapproval when he offered them to her.

"They were already trying to get out of the vineyard," he said in his defense. "I merely aided their escape."

She rubbed a grape between her fingers before tossing it into her mouth with a happy grin. He waited until she finished the grapes then took her hand. Eyes on the road, Miryam smiled as her slim fingers disappeared into his.

Miryam and Yosef encountered a row of kneeling camels assembled just outside the city gate when they arrived in Sepphoris. Loaders were busy taking cargo from a central pile and distributing it among the animals. The camels huzzed and grunted as their burdens increased.

A handler followed the loaders down the row checking each camel's bindings and testing the weight of their panniers, the pair of large wicker cargo baskets slung on either side of the animal. If he found them out of balance or under weight, he called for an adjustment.

They were searching for the caravan's leader when someone called out to Yosef. He turned and smiled when he saw a traveling merchant he knew heading toward them. Yosef sometimes sold him trays and other utensils that Kahlil resold in the markets of the towns he visited.

"Where are you working today?" Kahlil asked.

"No work for Yosef this morning." He rested his arm on Miryam's shoulder as he presented her to Kahlil. He introduced Kahlil to Miryam by saying, *Kahlil is the reason I am in Nazareth.*

Yosef showed him the bundle he carried. "I escorted my betrothed wife to Sepphoris so she can join your caravan. She will be going as far as Beth HaKerem."

Kahlil offered to put the package with his merchandise. He also promised to keep a watchful eye on Miryam as they traveled and see her safely lodged in the women's tent each evening.

The handler completed roping the camel train together. He barked a command and one-by-one the animals struggled to their feet, complaining as they rose.

Yosef led Miryam into the shade of a nearby tree. "How long will you be gone?"

"It depends upon Elisheva's needs."

"If you are still there for *Shavu'ot*, I will come and visit you. In the meantime, I will pray for you each morning and every evening and think of nothing but you in between."

"And I will do the same," Miryam replied.

Yosef brought out a small bag of coins tied at the top. He placed it in the palm of her hand and drew her other hand over it. "For your needs while we are apart." His lips quivered. "*Kol Tuv*, my wife."

She rested an arm on his shoulder and stepped closer. "May you also *Be Well,* my husband, while we are apart," she whispered then lifted her face for a good-bye kiss.

~ 16 ~

"Blessed are you among women, and blessed is the fruit of your womb!" ~ Luke 1:42

The trip to Beth Hakerem took the usual four-and-a-half days. However, Miryam's response to the trip was very different than it had been only weeks earlier when they followed the same route to Jerusalem for Pesach.

Though the caravan's pace was no faster than usual, Miryam could barely keep up. She had to force herself out of her bedroll each morning. Rather than greet the new day with vigor and enthusiasm, she inwardly groaned when she heard the gong at first light. By the time they called a midday halt to rest and eat, most of her energy reserves were sapped. She spent the afternoons plodding along like an over-burdened pack animal. After a long day of walking, she staggered into the women's tent and collapsed onto her bedroll in exhaustion.

She began to wonder if making this trip within mere weeks of the other one had been a mistake. This feeling of near constant exhaustion beset most newly pregnant women, although Miryam was unaware of it at the time. Like any young woman, Miryam understood the basic fundamentals of child-bearing. But she and her mother had never discussed the many changes that occur in a woman's body when she was with child.

Why should they? She was not even married yet.

In spite of its physical toll, the trip south did provide her the necessary solitude to ponder her circumstances and offer prayers for the Lord's help. She analyzed and re-analyzed her situation, mulling over the full ramifications of the angel's visit. Even this early in the process, she realized the utter impossibility of doing this with any certitude. She knew the full impact of her decision would slowly become clear, like a bud of a plant flowering. In the near term, she'd count on Elisheva. That was, after all, why she'd made the trip in the first place.

Elisheva was hanging clothes out to dry when Miryam crested the hill leading to Beth HaKerem. She turned when Miryam called to her. Recognizing her young cousin, she tossed the garments aside and hurried to greet her.

"Your family always visits at *Shavu'ot*, which is still six weeks away. Why are you so early?" Elisheva glanced around the front yard and down the road. "And where are your parents?"

"I came alone. As soon as I learned of your condition, I knew I must come to see you."

Elisheva's face registered both shock and surprise. She shook her cloak, trying to hide the swelling in her belly. "I have been careful to keep it a secret. How could you possibly have known I am with child?"

"An angel told me about you," Miryam said with a smile as they embraced.

A mighty wind moved over the face of the waters. It crossed the Judean Desert as they spoke. Streaking toward them, it raced across the dry plains raising swirling columns of sandy soil in its wake. Barley fields shivered as it passed and excitement rippled through the tall grasses in the parched wadis. Rising from the valley as an afternoon breeze, it swept around the two women, imparting wisdom, truth and knowledge.

Miryam tightened her veil around her head, Elisheva reached up to tuck wispy locks of gray hair back into place. She gasped when the babe in her womb leapt at the unexpected knowledge carried on the wind.

Elisheva took Miryam's hands in hers. "You are also with child," she said. "How is it that the mother of my Lord should come to me?"

"Like you, I must ask how you know this."

"The Spirit of the Lord came to me on the wind and the babe within me leaped for joy at the sound of your voice. You are truly blessed among women."

"My spirit rejoices in God my Savior, for he has regarded the low estate of his handmaiden," Miryam said in reply. "Whenever future generations speak of this, they will call me blessed for he who is mighty has done great things for me."

"You must be tired from your trip. Come inside and rest. Zecharias will not be home until suppertime." Elisheva said over her shoulder as she opened the door. "His absence will give us time to talk."

"I pity Zecharias," Miryam said when she'd emptied the glass of water her cousin gave her. The poor man must now live under one roof with two women both of whom are with child. Whatever will he say?"

Elisheva shook her head. "He will not say anything. The poor man no longer talks."

Miryam's brows knit together. "What happened?"

"An angel of the Lord appeared to him while he burned incense in the Temple. He is being punished because he questioned the angel's words."

"How long will this chastisement last?"

Elisheva shrugged. "We do not know when his voice will come back. Until it does, he communicates by writing little notes on a piece of slate he carries with him everywhere he goes." She glanced across the room. "What is in that package you brought?"

"It is a gift, a very special one for you and your baby. My betrothed husband, Yosef, is a carpenter. When I told him that you were with child and I planned to visit you, he made a cradle for your infant."

"So you are now betrothed. What part does this Yosef play in your visit?"

"None," Miryam said, firmly. "He does not even know I am with child."

"And when he finds out, what then?"

"I must trust the Lord and deal with it when the time comes."
Miryam crossed the room to get the package. She carried it over
and laid it on the kitchen table. "The cradle is in pieces. I will
show you how to assemble it."

"Tell me more about Zecharias and his encounter with the
angel," Miryam said as they sat admiring the cradle.

"He was beside himself by the time they brought him home.
He wouldn't eat any supper when I fixed it. You should have seen
his face. I have never seen anyone look so bereft and forlorn.
Nothing I said or did had any impact."

"He must have been devastated."

Elisheva nodded. "The sun went down and we got ready for
bed like any other night. Heaven knows Zecharias and I are not
young any longer. Still, I wanted him to know that no matter
what the angel did to him, I still loved him. So I started rubbing
his shoulders to help him relax."

A bright rosy glow crept over the old woman's cheeks. "And...
well, you know how it is with men and women. Without warning,
he suddenly rolled over, grabbed me and held me close. One
thing led to another and before I knew it, I was comforting him in
the way only a wife can comfort her husband."

Looking back on that evening brought a bemused smile to her
lips. "The night Zecharias returned from the Temple we came
together with an ardor neither of us had known for many a year."
Leaning close, she whispered, "Zecharias was not the only one
who grew inflamed with passion that night. I have not responded
like that since I was a young bride."

"Oh, my." Miryam nervously rocked the cradle as she
listened. "Well, uh, how very nice for you both."

"Sometimes the Lord does indeed work in mysterious ways."
Elisheva said with a wink. "You might say we were *inseparable*

for the next several days after the incident at the Temple." She patted Miryam's shoulder. "But then, you are betrothed; you understand about these things now."

Miryam bit her lip. "Actually, that is what I came to talk to you about.

Elisheva began arranging items on the kitchen counter in anticipation of fixing supper. "Motherhood has been a most interesting journey. It had not been for me as it is with women for a number of years. I never expected anything like this to happen. And, being past my prime, I did not experience one of the earliest of signs which tell a woman she is with child."

"How did you find out?"

"About six weeks after the incident at the Temple I woke up with an unsettled stomach. It continued day after day, until the day I became ill while preparing his morning meal and had to run outside" She frowned. "When I returned, I complained about being nauseous and my breasts becoming tender."

Zecharias ran his eyes up and down me and grinned. Reaching for his slate, he wrote, *"That is how it is when you are with child."*

"It seems that, in his rush to be *comforted*, he somehow forgot to tell me about the angel's promise of a son. He just assumed that, being a woman, I would somehow know. I could have swelled up like a wineskin full of new wine before he told me anything. And *that* is how I found out why the angel took his speech," she said with a derisive snort.

Miryam reached into her purse and removed the sack of coins Yosef gave her. Opening it, she counted out several and handed them to Elisheva. "Here is some of the money Yosef gave me when I left. It will help make up for the inconvenience of having another person in the house."

~ 17 ~

"She said, 'Pray, let me glean and gather among the sheaves after the reapers.' So she came, and she has continued from early morning until now, without resting even for a moment."
~ Ruth 2:7

A few weeks into her visit, Miryam rose early and set about making the day's bread while Elisheva washed and dressed.

She removed a large bowl for the dough from the cupboard and sat it on the table along with spoons and salt. She carried a cup to a crock in the corner, slid the lid aside and dipped out some starter. Leaving the starter on the counter, she tucked the mixing bowl under her arm and headed for the pantry.

For reasons Miryam didn't understand, the pantry seemed to be off limits to her. Elisheva had been somewhat secretive about its contents and made a point of personally gathering the ingredients for their meals. This was the first time Miryam entered the mysterious room and what she saw shocked her.

Bunches of dried herbs hung from the ceiling just as in the pantry at home. However, unlike her mother's pantry, the shelves were mostly bare. Her mouth dropped as she mentally cataloged Elisheva and Zecharias' meager provisions. She smiled when she noticed several bins and canisters in the corner.

Even without much else, there will still be grain for flour, and flour for bread.

Miryam opened a canister, leaned over, and stared into its dusty bottom. Had I known we were out of flour, I could have ground some grain last night, she thought. Putting her bowl aside, she removed the hand-powered flour mill from the shelf and carried it out to the kitchen. Now she would be ready to make the flour.

Returning to the pantry, she lifted the lid on the first grain bin. It was as empty as the canister. Most families kept a bin for wheat, one for spelt and a third, larger one, for barley. She moved on to the one beside it and found it empty as well. The final bin had a handful of barley kernels mingled with a few cracked pieces and some chaff. Miryam bent into the bin and used her hand to sweep the last of the barley into a little mound. She scooped the pitiful pile into her bowl and carried it out.

She was closing the pantry door behind her just as Elisheva entered the kitchen.

"What were you doing in my pantry?" Elisheva demanded. Her tone made it sound more like an accusation than a question.

"I thought I could help by starting the bread." She tilted the bowl toward her cousin. "But this is all the barley I could find. Where do you keep the rest?"

Elisheva sank onto a stool and buried her face in her hands. "There is no *rest*. That is all we have. Our barley is all gone." Salty tears rolled down the old woman's cheeks and dribbled onto her tunic, leaving dark spots. "We have nothing to eat. That is why I always went into the pantry. I did not want you to see how desperate our circumstances had become."

"Has this come about because Zecahrias cannot speak?"

Elisheva gave a sad nod in reply. "It is not his fault. People do not understand that being a priest limits what a man can do. The Law does not allow someone to be a common laborer part of the year and then put aside their work to go serve in the Temple when it is their turn." The timbre of her voice pleaded for Miryam's sympathy. "He must remain holy; he is required to separate himself from such worldly pursuits."

"How well did you get along when he could speak?"

"We were never wealthy, but we managed. He received a share of the offerings each time he served at the Temple. I worked the garden and tended the goats. He also preformed priestly duties here in the village, offering prayers for special intentions or thanksgivings, giving the blessing at circumcisions and marriages. Afterwards, people usually rewarded him with a jug of oil or wine, or some foodstuffs. Occasionally one of the landowners would give him a few coins."

Miryam stared into the empty bowl on the table between them. "And then he had his encounter with the Angel," she said with a disheartened shrug.

"Things went fairly well at first," Elisheva said. "Each Priestly Division serves twice a year. He, of course, received his full share for the time Gabri'el stole his voice. I was with child when Sukkoth came a little over two months later. He could not go, but they sent home a full share.

"The priests always receive less during the Festivals because there are so many of them on duty. That is another thing we learned to live with. His division served again in the month of Tevet, about three months after Sukkoth, and his brother priests again sent home a full share. However, at *Pesach* the assembly overrode his division and voted not to provide a share to Zecharias because his defect made it impossible for him to serve in the Temple."

Miryam bit her lip. "I had forgotten about the Laws regarding bodily defects which render a man unfit for priestly service."

Tears again glistened in Elisheva's eyes. She made a fist and pounded it on her knee. "If only there was some way of knowing when all of this will come to an end. The Angel made a number of prophecies. First, he said I would bring forth a son." She couldn't help but smile as she patted the bulge under her tunic. "And I am."

"Next he said our son would take the vow of a Nazarite. Then he spoke of him receiving the spirit of Elijah and leading Israel to the Lord. After striking Zecharias dumb, Gabri'el said, 'Because you did not believe my words you will be silent and unable to speak until the day that these things come to pass, which will be fulfilled in their time.'"

Elisheva's voice grew shrill. "When is that? When the baby is born? When he is grown? Will I even live long enough to hear Zecharias speak again?"

Her agitation proved contagious. Miryam sighed and rubbed her temples. "You have no chance of any of this coming to pass if you starve to death. Why not use the coins I gave you to buy a little food?"

"Yosef's coins are long gone," Elisheva said, staring into her lap. "I used them to buy the food we have been eating."

A look of horror crossed Miryam's face. "Then this is my fault." She reached out to Elisheva. "I am so sorry. It was never my intent to make things harder on you."

Elisheva took her hand and squeezed it. "Nonsense. We could not have survived this long without the money you brought. The Feast of *Shavu'ot* comes next month, though based on what happened after *Pesach*, they will not send us anything. Our only hope is that the priestly division of Abijah does not abandon us. Yet even if they do send us a portion when they are on duty again, we face two months without food."

"There is only one answer," Miryam said resolutely.

Elisheva shook her head. "No. How would it look if a priest sat at the Temple gate with a begging bowl? Zecharias would sooner starve to death...and I do not blame him."

"No one has to beg. They are harvesting the barley crop right now. I will go into the fields and glean for you."

Lifting her chin, Elisheva shook her head. "No, I cannot let you do that. This is my dilemma, not yours. If anyone has to become a gleaner, it should be me."

Miryam crossed her arms and gave her a searing frown. "You and I both know that is impossible. Your baby is due just after *Shavu'ot*. You are already so big you can barely reach down to tie your sandals. I am the only one who can do it, and I will."

"Who will protect you from the men?"

"I am the handmaiden of the Lord. He will protect me. If Ruth could do it, so can I." She punctuated the statement a definitive nod, closing the matter to further discussion.

~ **18** ~

"So she gleaned in the field until evening; then she beat out what she had gleaned..." ~ Ruth 2:17

Miryam had already left for the fields when Zecharias and Elisheva arose the following morning.

Elisheva dipped into the barley she borrowed the day before from a neighbor and set to work on the day's baking. Using the hand mill, she ground the barley into flour, then added starter and let the dough rise. When it was ready, she baked the loaves.

While the bread cooled, she drained the dried beans she'd left to soak overnight and added garlic and onion along with a few vegetables from the garden. She pushed the three-legged pot into the embers left from her baking and banked the coals around it.

Throughout the day, she paused at odd moments to ponder her young cousin hard at work in the hot sun and pray for her safety. Shadows lengthened as the afternoon sun began its slow descent into the horizon. Niggling worries crowded Elisheva's mind as the hours continued to pass without any sign of Miryam. The supper hour came and she dished up a bowl of stew for Zecharias, saying she would wait and eat with Miryam when she returned.

While her husband ate in silence, Elisheva nervously paced back and forth between the kitchen and the door, checking and rechecking the road. A burst of excitement rippled through her when, at long last, a shadowy figure materialized over the distant rise.

Heart pounding, she watched the person approach with bated breath. Bent under a heavy load, they rocked from side to side as they walked, struggling to maintain their balance.

"Please let it be Miryam," Elisheva whispered with clasped hands as she watched them turn off the main road and begin the slow climb up the hillock leading to the village of Beth HaKerem.

Squinting into the setting sun, she at last recognized familiar features hidden beneath the grime. A few moments later, Miryam paused at the stoop, swung the heavy burlap bag off her shoulder, and plopped it down at Elisheva's feet.

"This barley will keep us in bread for a good while," Miryam said, rolling her shoulders to ease out the kinks. She swept a sleeve across her forehead, spreading a dark smear across her sunburned face. Despite her disheveled appearance and obvious fatigue, Miryam was in irrepressibly good spirits. She took a deep breath and grinned at her cousin. "You did not think I could do it, did you?"

"True, you brought home the barley, but at what cost? Look at you."

For the first time Miryam became aware of what she must look like. She undid the sweat-stained scarf she'd tied around her hair and snapped it out. A gust of evening breeze carried away a cloud of dust along with bits of straw and more than a few insects.

The tips of her fingers were black and she had dirt caked under the fingernails. Elisheva pushed back her sleeves and frowned at the scratches and scrapes on the back of Miryam's hands and forearms. Tears welled in the old woman's eyes when she turned those hands over. The day's labor had left Miryam's palms chapped and cracked.

"Go to your room and get out of those dirty clothes. I will draw water so you can wash. We'll put some olive oil and aloe on your hands and face after you have dressed. I made bread and cooked a pot of stew. The two of us can eat together."

Miryam motioned toward the sack in the corner as she sat down to supper. "The barley is threshed, but it still needs to be cleaned."

Elisheva filled their bowls and carried them to the table. "You have done enough. I will take care of the barley in the morning after I wash your clothing. You can spend the day resting."

Miryam broke her bread and used it to push stew into her spoon. "The foreman said they would be harvesting there for several more days. I will go back tomorrow and get some more."

"You should rest."

"There will be time to rest after the harvesters have moved on." She took a napkin and wrapped a loaf in it. "I will lay out a burlap bag before I go to bed so I can get an early start in the morning. I can eat this on my way to the fields."

Elisheva unfolded the napkin and added additional loaves. "I am not the only one in this family with a child in her womb. That baby you carry is more important than how much barley Elisheva has in her pantry." Her tone reminded Miryam of the way her mother sounded whenever she scolded.

"It is still early for me." Miryam pulled her tunic tight across her abdomen."See. It will be a number of weeks before I begin to show. Meanwhile, the barley is ripe and ready and I am the only one in the household who can gather it. I plan to leave you with a bin full of barley when I go back to Nazareth."

Miryam extended her bowl when Elisheva asked if she wanted more. "All that work made me hungry," she said sheepishly.

She used her last bit of bread to sop up the gravy. She glanced across the table, smiling as she chewed. "I almost forgot the best news. One of the workwomen told me they will begin harvesting wheat very soon. When I finish with the barley, I plan to ask about and see if someone will allow me to glean their wheat fields."

True to her word, Miryam continued to go into the fields and lugged home two additional bags of barley. Her hard work resolved Elisheva and Zecharias' immediate food crisis. After taking a few day's rest, she headed off again early in the morning with several loaves tucked into a napkin and an empty burlap sack under her arm in search of wheat.

The demand for barley exceeded that for wheat, meaning the area's farmers allocated fewer fields to wheat. It was also the last grain crop of the season. Combined, these two factors meant there were more gleaners competing for fewer leftovers. Despite the competition, Miryam persisted. She eventually managed to almost fill the wheat bin in Elisheva's pantry.

Miryam recapped her circumstances as she took her well-earned rest. She'd been with child for over a month already. The time had passed with amazing speed.

~ 19 ~

"You shall count for yourselves seven weeks; from when the sickle is first put to the standing crop shall you begin counting seven weeks. Then you will observe the Festival of Shavu'ot for the Lord, your God." ~ Deuteronomy 16:9-10

Over eight weeks earlier, in preparation for their coming trip to Jerusalem for the *Pesach*, Yoachim had lit a lamp and sat it near the center of the table. He unrolled a small papyrus scroll on the table top and moved it into the circle of light. Then he'd brought over a small flat dish of ink and a writing stylus.

Miryam tiptoed up behind him and rested a hand on her father's shoulder. "What are you doing, Abba?" she asked, in much the same way as she had when she was a little girl. They'd enacted this ritual for many years.

He'd grinned. "I am making the sheet on which I will count the *Omer*." He lifted his eyes from his work. "Would you like to watch?"

Miryam slid a chair over and sat beside him. "If you are sure you will not mind." She rested her elbow on the table. Cupping her chin, she leaned forward to see.

"I never mind having you near. A great void will enter my life the day you leave us." The words caught in his throat. He'd told her this same thing since she was very small. Now, for the first time, those poignant words had real meaning. She will be Yosef's wife next *Pesach* with a home of her own, he thought. Turning aside, he quietly blotted the corner of his eye with his sleeve.

Like always, he and Miryam chatted as he worked. Knowing this was the last time she'd sit beside him as he worked, Yoachim collected each moment, storing every word and nuance in his memory like a miser gathering his gold.

Her father followed a routine honed over many years. He tested the ink after each stroke making sure it was dry before moving on. He repeated the tedious process of work and wait, work and wait, until he'd drawn eight horizontal lines on his scroll. He added vertical lines next, creating seven columns. He would use this grid to keep track of the days and weeks as he fulfilled the Torah command to count the *Omer*, the days until the Festival of *Shavu'ot,* or as many called it, *Pentecost.*

Another task completed for the trip to Jerusalem, he thought, with a satisfied smile. He placed the scroll on a high shelf to dry over night, kissed Miryam on the forehead, and left to prepare for bed. Yoachim rose early the following morning and inspected the scroll. Satisfied, he tied it with a ribbon and tucked it into his satchel so he'd have it when they arrived in Jerusalem.

Counting the *Omer* began the day after Passover and he wanted his sheet near at hand when they celebrated the Festival of Unleavened Bread. On the second day of Passover, they cut an *omer* of barley and brought it to the Temple as a harvest offering. They referred to this grain offering as the *Omer.*

Right on schedule, Yoachim rose on the day after Passover and recited the required prayer before supper. Then he proudly produced his scroll for all to see and announced, "This is the first day of the *Omer.*" Having fulfilled the Torah commands, he lined through the first box with gusto. He would continue this daily ritual of calling out the accumulated count and marking off another day for the next seven weeks.

As time passed, the little papyrus scroll became smudged and tattered. When Miryam left to visit Elisheva, Anna noticed a definite lack of enthusiasm in her husband's proclamations. He'd lost the most important part of his audience. All he had left now was Anna and Yosef when he visited. The two of them ignored the deteriorating condition of the scroll and instead saw the daily announcements as a way of measuring the time until they'd see Miryam again.

To make certain he'd accompany them on their trip to Jerusalem, Anna visited Yosef's shop as the final week of the

Omer counting drew near. Now officially part of the family, he readily agreed. As usual, they planned to stay with Anna's cousin, Elisheva, and her husband, Zecharias, during the Festival.

Because *Shavu'ot* started on the fiftieth day after *Pesach,* both celebrations began on the same day of the week. Knowing this allowed the pilgrims to schedule their trip so as to accommodate the Torah command against travel on the *Shabbat,* yet still arrive on time.

The family followed the same route as they had when they went up to Jerusalem for *Pesach.* This time, however, there was a special urgency in the footsteps. It'd been more than six weeks since Miryam left and, although no one voiced it, all three of them missed her greatly.

Miryam came out of the bedroom adjusting her clothes. She glanced over at Elisheva, turned sideways, and asked, "How do I look?"

"You did a wonderful job. The new tunic fits perfectly."

"I meant do I look as if I am with child?" She snatched up a cloak and shoved her arms into it. "What if I wore a cloak over it? Is this better?"

"How many times do I have to tell you? It is too early for anyone to tell."

Miryam swiveled at the waist and pretended to reach for a high shelf. "Do you see how tight it is when I stretch? Everyone will surely notice."

Elisheva crossed the room and put her arm around her young cousin's shoulder. "Over the next week you will encounter three groups of people: strangers, neighbors and family. The strangers are of no concern. Since they do not know you, they will pay you no attention. Our neighbors have already grown accustomed to seeing you come and go. They have other things on their mind. Lastly, you will be interacting with family members. These are the people who see you through the eyes of love. We see you for what you are, not how you look."

"But when you have been away from someone for a time, you notice little changes, slight changes."

"Most women add a little weight prior to their monthly cycle. Do you expect any of them to be brazen enough to ask about it?"

Miryam frowned and shook her head.

Elisheva took her by the hand and led her into the kitchen. They sat at the table opposite each other, each resting an arm on the tabletop. "Why is it so important that no one know you are with child? You did not have any problem talking to me about it."

"I came here because I needed to share my story with someone who has had a somewhat similar experience."

"And you fear their reaction might not be the same as mine. These people *love* you, Miryam."

The young woman sighed. "I *will* tell them, just not right now. After all, it is hardly something I can keep hidden forever. I just want to do it when the time is right."

Rising, she walked to the door and stared down the road hoping to see them, yet somehow relieved when she didn't.

"You can stare out at that road until your eyes fall out, but it will not make them get here a moment sooner," Elisheva said as Miryam sank back into her chair.

~ 20 ~

The trip to Jerusalem had been full of laughter, anticipation and excitement. Now the same, but much more somber, group slogged home speaking only when necessary.

Another *Shavu'ot* had come and gone, Yosef thought as he walked. They'd performed the same rites, recited familiar prayers and renewed old friendships. A week's worth of memories were quickly stored away, joining other, older ones as images of home pushed them aside. He had looked forward to *Shavu'ot*, welcoming the respite the Festival provided. He was also grateful for the opportunity to introduce Miryam to his family.

Leaving her behind was the most painful thing he'd ever done. Remembering her standing in the doorway waving good-bye was like ripping the covering off of a partially healed wound. Since she left Nazareth for Beth HaKerem, thoughts of Miryam filled his days and haunted his nights.

He stared at the distant horizon and tried to imagine what she was doing at that moment. He wondered if he would ever understand Miryam's compelling need to stay behind with Cousin Elisheva. There was something both Miryam and Elisheva took pains to conceal from him. Of that much, he was certain.

He sensed an indefinable change in Miryam, change he couldn't quite put his finger on. What this secret was and why they found it necessary to hide it from him, he couldn't say. Not knowing allowed his imagination to run wild. Were he less secure in her love for him he might be tempted to question her fidelity. He forced the notion from his mind. He refused to even consider Miryam capable of such an atrocity.

Yosef accompanied Anna and Yoachim on the return trip to Nazareth. Traveling together, sharing meals, rising and resting when they did allowed them all to become better acquainted. And, since it was just the three of them, it gave Yosef the opportunity to observe their interactions close up.

The more time he spent with them, the more his respect for his new parents grew. What impressed him most was the depth of their love. He couldn't help wondering if his own parents had enjoyed a similar relationship. If they did, he'd been so much a part of it that he failed to appreciate it.

The years had blended and bonded Anna and Yoachim to such an extent that neither was complete without the other. Whenever they thought he wasn't looking, their fingers found each other's in the evening shadows around the campfire.

Anna had never been the fruitful vine within Yoachim's house that the Psalms spoke of. They both accepted it as God's will and tried not to dwell on it. Instead of children like olive shoots around the table, they had only one, Miryam. She'd come to them late in life, bringing joy to them both. Despite the embarrassment it sometimes caused him, Anna and Yoachim were not shy about mentioning the potential expansion of their little family. At times, it seemed to him they spoke of little else other than the anticipated arrival of grandchildren.

Yosef switched the strap of his pack onto the other shoulder. One more night on the road and they'd be home, he thought with a sigh. Like it or not, he needed to put thoughts of Miryam aside and focus on his work. His Jewish neighbors accepted the necessity to abandon the demands of one's occupation and journey to Jerusalem for the Festivals. His Gentile customers, by comparison, were generally confused by the whole process and failed to make such allowances.

Yosef was still trying to get on top of his backlog when Anak dropped in to pay a visit. He was his usual self, full of energy, opinionated and nosy. "So, how was Jerusalem? When did you get back? Why have you not dropped by to see me? Where have you been keeping yourself?"

"Jerusalem was very good. We arrived home two days ago, and I have not left my shop since."

"What were you doing?

"I had many things to take care of, mostly orders for customers in Sepphoris."

Anak raised his eyebrows and motioned with his hands as if he were pulling words out of Yosef's mouth. "You are gone a week and all can say is '*orders for Sepphoris?*'"

He sat his tools aside. "I traveled with Imma Anna and Abba Yoachim. In addition to visiting the Temple and offering sacrifice, I met Anna's cousin, Elisheva, and her husband, Zecharias, in Beth HaKerem. Miryam is staying with her, so it enabled me to have some time alone with my betrothed wife."

Yosef smiled for the first time. "We left her parents in Beth HaKerem and went away by ourselves. I took her to Bethlehem where she met some of my family. We stayed over there for one night."

"*We stayed over there for one night*? You said it so innocently, so matter-of-factly. What a sly fox you are." Anak said, chuckling."

Yosef frowned. "I do not understand what you mean."

Anak lifted his hands in an elaborate shrug. "We are friends. There is no need to feign ignorance with me. Staying over in another village forced the two of you to share a room." He stared at the rafters overhead, and thinking out loud said, "I must remember that ploy."

"Do not allow your imagination to run wild. I stayed with my brother and Miryam slept at my sister's home."

Anak shook his head in disgust. "I was right when I said you are hopeless. Fate presents you with a lovely opportunity, and you waste it." He walked to the door, threw it open and stuck his head out. "Miryam has no carpentry business to look after, why have I not seen her about town?"

"She is still at Cousin's Elisheva's home. She will come back when her tasks there are complete."

"And that was that?" Anak snapped his fingers. "Some husband you are. Since when does the wife make the decisions?"

"We discussed her trip before she left. Once Elisheva has her baby, Miryam will return."

Narrowing his eyes, Anak cupped his chin and stared at Yosef. "Could there be some other reason Miryam wants to stay in Judea? Perhaps she has met someone in Jerusalem, someone more interesting, perhaps a little wealthier than the simple carpenter she left behind in Nazareth."

Righteous anger flared in Yosef's eyes. He threw down his tools and roared out from behind his workbench. "How dare you slander my wife!" he shouted as he grabbed Anak.

Yosef slammed him against the wall before Anak had a chance to respond. His eyes widened with fear when he saw the color rising in Yosef's face and neck. Realizing he was no match for the furious carpenter, he began sputtering apologies.

"This time you have gone too far. I will not allow you or anyone else to sully Miryam's reputation." Yosef's straight left arm pinned his hapless victim to the wall. He reared back and cocked his fist.

Anak turned his face aside and scrunched up his eyes in anticipation of the coming blow.

Instead of punching him, Yosef unexpectedly released him. "I am sorry. I should not have lost my temper, but I could not tolerate any more of your intimations. Why must you always take things too far?"

Anak continued to cower, not saying a word.

Still breathing hard and shaking with anger, Yosef took another step back. He rolled his shoulders and apologized again.

Anak flinched when Yosef reached out to smooth his rumpled cloak.

"I think it would be best for both of us if you left me to my work now," Yosef quietly said.

Anak gave a quick nod and dashed out the door, scurrying away without another word.

Yosef's hands were still not steady when he returned to his bench. Confident that hard work was the best remedy; he picked up his plane and ran it across the board. It only took an instant for him to realize something was terribly wrong.

His heart sank when he flipped the plane over. He'd knocked the blade askew when he slammed it down to grab Anak. This misaligned corner of the blade left a deep gouge across the center of the board. A momentary lapse had destroyed his work.

Grabbing a mallet, Yosef tapped out the bench dogs securing the panel. He briefly considered throwing the board across the room, but thought better of it. At the very least he could cut it down and make drawer fronts out of it on another day.

He stared off into the distance and rubbed his throbbing temples. Why had Anak's words infuriated him so? Yosef wondered.

Could it be, Yosef wondered, that Anak had spoken aloud what he had already been thinking?

~ 21 ~

Miryam moved along the garden row on her knees, picking the ripe bean pods and accumulating them in her apron. After they were shelled, they'd spread them on a thin cloth to dry in the sun. She grunted when her knee encountered a hidden rock. Poking her fingers into the loose soil, she dug it out with her hand and pitched it across the yard.

She mused over her situation as she worked her way down the row. Elisheva's time drew closer with each passing day. She'd come to Beth HaKerem immediately after her encounter with the angel, Gavri'el, because she felt Elisheva was the only one who could truly relate to her situation.

That was true as far as it went, Miryam thought. Even though Elisheva was barren and past child bearing age, thanks to a miraculous intervention she was now with child. Similar things had occurred in the lives of Avraham and Sarah, and Elkanah and Channah. Clearly the hand of the Almighty had been directing each of their destinies.

While her maternity and these others hinged upon divine intervention, there were as many differences between them as there were similarities. Sarah brought forth Isaac, one of the Patriarchs of the Jewish nation. Channah birthed Samuel, a great prophet who shepherded the nation into the Davidic Monarchy. And now Elisheva would soon give birth to the forerunner of the *Mashiach*.

Miryam imagined the flow of time as a mighty river, always moving relentlessly forward as it sought its ultimate end. All of history has been building to this moment, she thought.

But all three of them, Elisheva, Channah and Sarah, were *married women*. They all had a husband who lay with them and implanted the seed of future life. She, by comparison, was the one who had never known a man, the virgin of whom Isaiah had spoken and to whom the angel testified. Truly, hers was an event she could never truly share with another. Many women had given birth to great and noble sons, but only one would give birth to the *Mashiach*. There would never be another like her.

Despite the hot sun, she shivered. "My little *Mashiach*," she whispered, gazing down at the hand she'd automatically placed over her womb. "Some equally great and frightening things surely await us. May my love always surround you, and may yours surround me with the courage needed for what lies ahead.

Folding up the corners of her apron, Miryam rose and brushed away the dirt on her knees before letting her tunic drop around her ankles. She clutched the apron against her as she walked back to the house. She looked forward to spending time working in the kitchen with Elisheva, and frequently sought her insights when they did.

Just after the family left to return to Nazareth Miryam had felt a strange fluttering sensation in her abdomen. Worried that something might be wrong, she hurried to seek Elisheva's advice. On hearing her concerns, her older cousin smiled and hugged her. "You have nothing to fear. Every mother experiences it. It is the quickening. The baby has begun moving within your womb."

She was entering the *in-between time* as Elisheva's friends called it. The numbing tiredness that beset most women during the first months of child bearing had slipped away unnoticed. Examining herself when she bathed, Miryam saw the telltale rounding of the child growing within her womb, but the latter time when the size of the child within made everyday tasks difficult was still several months away.

The next morning Miryam was milking the goats when she heard the door slam. Looking up, she saw Zecharias standing at the back door desperately swiveling his head. Having learned that the years had dimmed his sight, she waved her hand in the air and called, "Over here. I am with the goats."

The old man's robes billowed as he raced toward her. In his rush to get to her, he'd left the house without the slate tablet he used to write on. He arrived wide-eyed and breathless and did an elaborate pantomime in an effort to get his message across.

Miryam quickly deciphered his actions. Elisheva's time had come. They returned to the house together and, after checking in on her cousin, Miryam left to notify the midwife.

Elisheva's baby boy came into the world later that day.

They took their infant to the local synagogue for his circumcision when he was eight days old. Friends and neighbors, all dressed in their finest garb, joined the parents in an alcove for this most special day. The man performing the operation, the *mohel,* was already there when they arrived.

Their designated *sandek,* the village elder Zecharias and Elisheva chose to hold the boy during the procedure, waited beside the arched entrance to the alcove. Befitting the honor bestowed upon him, the *sandek* had visited the *mikvah* earlier that morning for cleansing in a ritual bath. He wore his finest outfit and refrained from eating prior to the ceremony to further purify himself.

The alcove held two chairs sitting against the east wall. The first, the *sandek's* seat, was just a standard everyday chair. The one beside it, the *Chair of Elijah,* had ornately carved legs and arms with plush cushions on its seat and back. Tradition designated the chair for the Prophet Elijah. Jews considered Elijah to have a special relationship with children since he brought the son of the widow at Zarephath back to life.

Before the ceremony began, the *sandek* took his position in the plain chair facing west. The *mohel* bent over him whispering last minute instructions on how to sit and the best way to hold the infant.

Zecharias walked to the entrance to the alcove and took the child from Elisheva and placed him on the seat of the *Chair of Elijah.* After several moments, a family friend lifted him from the chair and returned him to his father. Zecharias then sat the boy in the *sandek's* lap. In this way, the child had symbolically moved from Elijah's lap to that of the *sandek*.

When the *mohel* completed the rite of circumcision, another family friend removed the wailing infant from the *sandek's* lap and passed him to the one designated to hold the baby boy for the blessings and naming ritual.

Knowing that Zecharias was unable to speak, the person tasked with naming the baby left the alcove and approached Elisheva. "You wish to name the boy Zecharias, correct?" he quietly asked,

Elisheva vigorously shook her head. "No! The child is to be called Yohan."

Everyone around her overheard and gasped.

Trying to maintain decorum, the leader of the synagogue stepped between them and whispered to Elisheva, "You are without a doubt mistaken. No one in his family has ever had that name. I will tell them to declare the boy *Zecharias* as he father most surely wishes."

Elisheva grabbed the arm of the man's robe when he started to turn away. Putting her face inches from his, she stared him in the eye and said, "We will settle this right now. Give Zecharias a writing tool."

The man rolled his eyes and muttered something about women interfering with the ceremonies as he left to get a slate and stick of charcoal.

Zecharias grabbed the slate out of his hand and wrote in letters large enough for even a blind man to read, "His name is Yohan."

Elisheva looked at her husband and gave him a wide smile.

The *sandek* hosted a festive meal after the ceremony to celebrate the admission of a new child into the covenant of Avraham.

After months of silence, Zecahrias found that he suddenly had his voice back and he had something to say to each and every person there.

Nestling the babe against her bosom, Elisheva indicated to Miryam that the time had come for them to leave. They paused when they reached the end of the village square and cocked their heads. They could still hear Zecharias chattering away in the distance. The two women looked at each other for an instant then covered their mouths to muffle their snickers. They continued chuckling as they hurried home to put him little Yohan to bed.

~ 22 ~

"And his father Zechari'ah was filled with the Holy Spirit, and prophesied, saying," ~ Luke 1:67

The sun was setting by the time Zecharias returned from the village. He trudged up the gravel path leading to their simple home, head bowed and deep in thought.

Elisheva heard his footsteps on the walk and put aside her preparations for their evening meal. Grabbing a towel to dry her hands, she hurried to the door to greet him.

He shuffled past her as if she wasn't there. Crossing the room without a word, Zecharias gave a long sigh and eased his weary bones into a chair.

The happy grin slipped from Elisheva's face as an eerie stillness descended upon the house. It suddenly felt as if nothing had changed.

Miryam remained in the small kitchen with baby Yohan asleep in the beautiful cradle Yosef had made. She peeked around the corner, watching the drama unfold.

Elisheva twisted the towel in her hands as she waited for him to speak. When Zecharias remained in the dark room with his head in his hands saying nothing, she tiptoed away and returned to the kitchen.

"He is just as he was before," she whispered to Miryam, "distant and mute. This morning, he could speak again. It felt as though our life had returned to normal. And now this."

Pent-up tears slowly trickled down Elisheva's face. Turning aside, she sniffed and dried her face with the towel. "In his jubilation could he have done or said something while he was with the men?" she wondered aloud. "Perhaps he made an offhanded comment, or did some little thing that offended the angel." She grabbed Miryam's hands in hers. "Could he have been struck dumb a second time?"

Miryam whispered an urgent prayer that Elisheva's fears not be true. "Did you speak to him when he came in?"

Elisheva shook her head. "The strange way he acted when he came in unnerved me. I was too frightened to do or say anything."

"Well, one way or another we will know soon enough," Miryam said as they resumed their work. They labored in silence, each lost in their own thoughts. Neither woman heard the old man's shuffling footsteps as he approached the kitchen doorway.

Elisheva spun around when she heard Zecharias' voice behind her. "I want both of you to come and sit with me."

She scooped the infant into her shaky arms and adjusted his blanket while Miryam lit a small lamp. Elisheva bent to kiss her husband's rough cheek before taking a seat beside him.

"Something weighs heavily on your heart. What is it my love?"

He touched her hand, but did not answer. His eyes had the appearance of someone seeing a world far beyond the here and now. After what seemed like an interminable wait, Zecharias turned to Miryam. The old man's weathered face crinkled when he smiled.

"You will be leaving us soon," he said with sadness. "If I could keep you here, I would. But the Lord has ordained another path for you and it awaits your footsteps even as we speak. He blessed her, saying, "Having you here has turned our humble home into a temple. Be safe, my child. You carry the hope of the world within you."

He patted her knee as he spoke. "Blessed be the Lord, the God of Israel. He has come to his people and set them free. He has raised up for us a mighty Savior, born of the house of his servant David. Through his holy prophets he promised of old, that he would save us from our enemies, from the hand of all who hate us. He promised to show mercy to our fathers and to remember his holy covenant.

"This was the oath he swore to our father Avraham: to set us free from the hands of our enemies, free to worship him without fear, holy and righteous in his sight all the days of our life."

Zecharias paused. He turned and extended his hands to his wife, asking for the infant.

Outside, the sky had grown dark. A full moon hung over the eastern mountains and a silvery shaft of moonlight illuminated the three of them as they sat in a tight circle.

Elisheva tenderly placed the slumbering babe into his father's hands. He lifted the child to the heavens and mouthed a silent prayer of thanksgiving to the God of the universe. He lowered the child to his lap, cradling his tiny week-old son in both hands while he lovingly stared down at him.

The boy's eyes suddenly popped opened as if on command. Ignoring Elisheva, the babe's focus remained on the man above him whose voice he had never heard. Time seemed to stop as father and son quietly stared into each other's eyes.

Zecharias began to speak to the boy. "You, my child, shall be called the prophet of the Most High. For you will go before the Lord to prepare his way, to give his people knowledge of salvation by the forgiveness of their sins. In the tender compassion of our God, the dawn from on high shall break upon us to shine on those who dwell in darkness and to guide our feet into the way of peace."

The holy moment came to an end. The baby's eyes fluttered and closed. Zecharias nestled him against his chest and softly rocked him back to sleep. The two women closed the circle, each resting an arm on the old man's shoulder.

~ 23 ~

Elisheva nursed the baby after breakfast while Miryam washed dishes. Alone in the small kitchen, Miryam allowed her mind to wander. The time of her visitation was drawing to a close, she thought with a hint of sadness. Being in Beth HaKerem had provided the two of them with sufficient time to discuss all that needed to be resolved.

Her thoughts turned to Nazareth and home. She missed Yosef and her parents terribly, especially after spending the week during Shavu'ot with them. Adding her travel time to the weeks she'd spent in Beth HaKerem meant that Miryam would have been away four months by the time she returned. Her tunic now strained against the small, but undeniable swelling of her abdomen.

It was tempting to imagine staying on in Beth HaKerem. Here she felt accepted, and more importantly, understood. Whenever people noticed the ring on her finger and her obvious pregnancy, they would smile and congratulate her.

What would life in Nazareth be like for her when she returned? Her friends and neighbors, who knew the whole truth, would undoubtedly have a very different response.

Now that he could talk again, Zecharias could take his place in the priestly rotation and earn a living again. But that was still several weeks off and Miryam knew well the sad state of their pantry. It was time for her to leave. With one less mouth to feed, Elisheva and Zecharias could eke their way along for the next few weeks until his division was on duty at the Temple.

Besides, she thought with a wistful smile, Yosef waited for her in Nazareth. She missed his company and looked forward to seeing him. Would he be as eager to see her, especially when he learned of her condition?

It would not be a problem once she explained things to him. She'd felt a sense of abiding peace and deep joy ever since the

morning she'd acquiesced to the Angel's request. Pushing the
negative thoughts from her mind, Miryam resumed drying the
dishes.

They'd completed all of the household tasks by mid-morning.
Elisheva slipped the slumbering infant into a pouch sling and
they headed off to visit traveling caravans in the hopes of finding
one that could take Miryam back home. It was only a short
distance from Beth HaKerem to the open plain where nomadic
merchants assembled their baggage trains.

The chatter of multiple foreign tongues echoed around the
two women as they walked along the thoroughfare of beaten-
down grass. Tents of various sizes lay scattered across the plain
in distinct groups. The vendors who made up the caravan and
their families, along with the drovers, camel boys and
roustabouts formed a sort of village.

Caravans from near and far came and left on a more or less
continuous cycle. When arriving, the caravan's leader surveyed
the available spots. Depending upon the time of year, they could
choose among many or race to claim the last remaining plot of
ground. Once they found an open parcel, they tethered the
animals, erected tents, and claimed the space as theirs.

A few days later, with their business concluded, the
merchants pulled up stakes and headed off to their next stop.
Often as not, the space they'd vacated became someone else's
home before its former occupant reached their next destination.

Miryam nervously examined the various groups encamped
there. She immediately eliminated several from consideration
because of their coarse language and the rough, unkempt
appearance of the men. She studied the remaining vendors,
trying to decide which ones to approach. Her first stop turned out
to be a disappointment. When asked, the man shook his head
and said he would be heading south along the Via Maris to Egypt
at morning's first light.

Her next stop was also unfruitful. This group planned to head for Idumea then go east past Lake Asphaltitis and on to Nabatea. She and Elisheva were walking away when the man called to them.

"Try Eumenes," he hollered when they looked back, and pointed to an encampment near the plateau's edge. "He is on his way back to Antioch and usually stops in Sepphoris."

The two women thanked him with a smile and a wave. Turning, they followed a well-worn dirt path that threaded its way through the maze of wagons and corrals of camels. Miryam grabbed Elisheva's hand as they drew closer to Eumenes' camp.

"See the group of young women sitting beside that tent," she said, leaning close and lowering her voice. "This is a good sign. If I travel with this caravan, I would have company. On my way to Beth HaKerem all of the unaccompanied women lodged together in a single tent. Yosef's friend, Kahlil, acted as our guardian and placed his bedroll outside the tent's entrance each night. This caravan must have a similar system."

They found Eumenes with one of his men, working on a wagon wheel. Seeing them approach, he handed the man under the wagon a tub of grease and walked over to meet them.

"We seek a man called Eumenes," Miryam said.

He gave a grunt of acknowledgement. "You have found him. Are you selling or buying?"

"Neither." Twisting halfway around, Miryam pointed back the way they'd come. "The merchant with the colorful wagons said you would probably stop at Sepphoris on your way to Antioch."

Eumenes picked his teeth with a fingernail. "True enough. We always pass through Sepphoris before heading north on the *Via Maris*."

"I would like to book passage as far as the Nazareth turnoff."

"For the two of you?"

"No," Miryam replied, "just for me."

He quoted her a figure slightly less than she'd paid coming to Beth HaKerem.

Delighted with the price, she asked, "How long do you allow for the trip?"

"Five and one half days. We will pass Nazareth in mid-afternoon." He shook his head when Miryam opened her money sack. "We leave the first day of the week; pay me the morning we leave. That way, if you change your mind or arrive after we have left, no harm is done."

Miryam smiled and turned aside to leave.

Eumenes' voice called her back. "Just so we understand each other...the amount I quoted you buys your safety. Bandits will not bother a caravan as large as mine. You will walk, and I do not slow my pace to accommodate stragglers. The animals get regular breaks. You may rest when they do. If there is space in a wagon and you wish to ride, you will have to negotiate the cost with that merchant."

Miryam's reply was firm and confident. "I made the same arrangements coming from Sepphoris and was able to keep up. I will plan to see you on the first day of the week."

"We will be here," he said and returned to continue working on the wagon wheel.

"Are you sure you have enough to pay the man?" Elisheva asked as they weaved their back across the field.

"I will have a wee bit left after I pay him." She read the expression on Elisheva's face and quickly added. "Which is alright. I will not have any need for money. My passage will be paid, I'll have a tent to sleep in and I can eat with the help just as when I came to Beth HaKerem."

~ 24 ~

The family rose before sunrise on the first day of the week. After a quick meal, Elisheva and Zecharias accompanied Miryam to meet the caravan. When Eumenes called for all wagons ready, Zecharias gave her a brief hug then quickly stepped aside.

Tears poured from Elisheva's eyes as she approached her. "I feel as if I am saying good-bye to my daughter," she sobbed. She squeezed Miryam tightly and kissed her several times.

"You made all the difference in my life. I can never repay you for everything you did for me," Miryam said as she returned her kisses. "I will remember our time together with fondness."

She stopped Elisheva when she began to back away. Miryam pulled the carrying pouch aside and leaned in to plant a kiss on Yohan's little forehead."

Falling into line, Miryam waved as they left the open plain heading north. Feeling like herself again, Miryam saw the trip back to Nazareth as manageable despite the weight of the child she carried. Certainly easier than the journey to Beth HaKerem, she thought with a smile.

Her thoughts briefly turned to the family visit they had during *Shavu'ot* as she walked. Had she been duplicitous in not telling anyone about her situation? What would Yosef have done if the situation were reversed? She frowned at the foolishness of such a notion. Yosef was a man; he could never *be with child.*

But a tiny voice in the back of her mind asked, *What if he fathered a child?*

She laughed to herself. That was completely different. The only way he could father a child would be to lie with another woman, someone not his wife. If he did that, Yosef would be guilty of the sin of adultery and subject to punishment under the Law of Moshe.

Miryam's hands protectively caressed the miraculous child

growing within her as icy fingers of fear climbed her spine.

What if that is what Yosef thinks I did?

Up ahead, the band of travelers slowed as they crested the top of the first hill. She drew a deep, cleansing breath and cast a backward glance at Jerusalem as it disappeared from view. Miryam adjusted the strap of her bag on her shoulder as she walked and recalled the happy memories of her time spent in Beth HaKerem. Though she'd ostensively come to Beth HaKerem to assist Cousin Elisheva, in fact, she was the one in need of assistance. Her time in Beth HaKerem had been a rewarding experience. Free to be herself, with Elisheva's help, she'd gradually come to grips with the phenomena overtaking her.

Despite her apprehensions, Miryam was glad to be heading home. She was going back to those she loved, returning to the place where she belonged. Her heart ached for Yosef and her parents. The very idea of seeing them all again sent a surge of energy through her. Head high, she marched on with renewed vigor.

They made good time, and by midmorning the caravan was nearing the Jericho road. Miryam watched the familiar landscape pass by. Seeing a particular rocky outcropping here, or a gnarled tree there, brought a happy smile of remembrance to her face. She'd made pilgrim trips to Jerusalem with her parents many times along this same route. She wiped away beads of sweat on her forehead. The rest stop the caravan would surely make before turning east to begin the long trek up the slope leading to Jericho would be a welcome respite.

An uneasy feeling welled-up inside her when the wagons didn't slow as she anticipated. Suddenly confused, she glanced around trying to make sense of the situation. Unbelievably, the entire caravan marched past the turnoff without stopping. Unaware of their mistake, they continued plodding northward. Fear rose in her throat as she watched the Jericho road slip away behind them.

How could they have failed to recognize this critical junction?

When no one sounded the alarm, Miryam knew she must act. Taking the initiative, she stepped out of line and jogged ahead. Weaving between the carts and camels, she gradually made her way to Eumenes' wagon at the head of the train. Running alongside him, she waved her arms and hollered for him to stop.

Eumenes glanced down at the frantic person beside his wagon, waving and screaming. He shook his head, frowned, and muttered a curse. Raising an arm high in the air, he shouted a command, signaling a halt. Pulling back on the reins, he slowed the team. When his wagon rolled to a stop, he set the brake. The other wagons, pack animals and travelers bunched up behind and around him, blocking the road.

He glared down at her. "What is so important that you must halt the entire caravan?"

Miryam's heart pounded from the run. She pressed her chest and gasped for breath. When she recovered enough to speak, she said, "We passed the turnoff to Jericho. I wanted to catch you as soon as possible. We can backtrack now without losing much time."

"And you stopped everyone to tell me this?"

"I knew you would want to know. I have traveled between Jerusalem and Nazareth many times and know the route well. Turning around now will save us much time and effort."

Eumenes leaned around the wagon's canvas canopy. Winking over at his second in command, he said, "This young woman thought we would appreciate knowing we rolled right past the Jericho turnoff."

"Thank her for me," his assistant shouted back with a grin. "I was so busy with the camels I did not even notice."

"What shall we do to reward her for this effort?"

Miryam gazed up at him. "Oh, that is not necessary. Knowing I have been of assistance is reward enough," she said with a modest smile.

"Your information would be very helpful," Eumenes said, "*if* we were heading to Jericho." He scowled down at her from the wagon's bench. "But, since we have no intention of going to Jericho, you've wasted everyone's time with your false alarm." He snapped the reins. "Now get back into line where you belong so we can continue on to *Samaria*."

Miryam's eyes widened. "I did not want to go through Samaria. When you said you were heading to Sepphoris, you never said anything about Samaria."

"You never asked." Eumenes said with a shrug. "There's still time to go back to the Jericho turnoff."

His second in command watched the interchange and snickered. He turned to the men beside him and whispered something. They nudged each other and pointed to Miryam. The news spread from one group to another, until the entire caravan joined in the laughter.

Harmonia, the sole woman among the merchants, silently watched the young traveler trudge to the back of the line, head bowed against the group's ridicule.

Ignoring the snickers of those around her, Miryam took her place at the end of the line as the caravan rolled on to Samaria. A woman dare not travel the road to Jericho alone.

The animals and the road intervened as more pressing tasks displaced the moment of temporary merriment. The chatter and laughter gradually subsided, lost amid the dust and rhythmic jingle jangle of the wagons. They'd forgotten the incident by the time they stopped to rest and water the animals.

The cook opened his stores and people began to eat their noonday meal. Still chastened by the group's laughter, Miryam retreated from the crowd and sat alone. She dug into her sack and brought out one of the loaves Elisheva had pressed into her hands that morning.

One of the roustabouts, a young man about her age, sought her out. Dropping onto the grass beside her, he glanced over and said, "It was an honest mistake; you meant well."

She didn't reply.

"Eumenes can be a brute at times. I have felt the lash of his sarcasm myself and know how his words can wound a person."

Miryam still made no comment.

"Do not allow him to ruin your trip." He smiled. "My name is Cerberus. What are you called?"

"Miryam," she said, staring at the ground.

"The cook had fresh dates." He extended his hand. "I took extra. Here, have a few."

She shook her head and nibbled her bread.

"I am offering to be your friend. It will be a long trip with no one to talk to."

"That is kind of you," she turned her hand, displaying the gold ring on her finger, "but not appropriate. You see, I have a husband."

Cerberus made a great show of carefully examining the members of the caravan lounging in the shade by the well. "I do not see him among the men. Where is he?"

"His name is Yosef and he awaits me in Nazareth."

"Since you are without husband and friends, Cerberus will look after you until we reach Nazareth." He gave her a sly smile. "Yosef need never know."

She smacked his hand away when he reached out to touch her. Stuffing the half-eaten loaf back into her bag, Miryam leaped up and hurried over to join the group at the well.

~ 25 ~

Following the route known as *The Way of Patriarchs,* the caravan arrived at their first stopover, Shiloh, late in the afternoon. Long ago overshadowed by Jerusalem to the south and Shechem to the north, Shiloh still retained remnants of art and architecture from times past. This was where Joshua gathered the tribes to declare victory, and where he cast lots, dividing the Promised Land. The Israelites erected the Tabernacle of the Lord here, and the Ark of the Covenant resided in Shiloh for 369 years before David the King transferred it to Jerusalem.

Miryam yearned to go into the city and wander among the sites, but fear of the Samaritans prevented her from doing it.

Eumenes had traveled this route many times before and knew the area well. Leaving the main road, he guided his wagon into a field within walking distance of the city walls. Harmonia followed his curving tracks through the grass. Veering aside at the last minute, she brought her wagon to a halt parallel to his. The thick grass would provide ample forage for the caravan's animals. The spot had a wide stream running through a gully behind a thicket of trees. The stream ensured ample water for travelers and animals alike.

Grateful for the opportunity to rest, Miryam walked over to a stand of mulberry trees. After shaking off the day's dust, she settled into the circle of shade beneath them. She sat on the ground with her back against a tree trunk, watching them set up camp.

What Miryam had called the *women's wagon,* driven by a man named Sarudi, creaked past and continued on for several hundred yards before stopping in an isolated spot.

Like Sarudi, the supply wagon also parked far from the center of camp. Two men jumped down carrying a heavy mallet and posts. They quickly laid out an expansive rectangle in the grassy field, driving posts as they went. Once they finished, Eumenes removed a large coil of rope from under his seat and strung it around the perimeter forming a makeshift corral.

Harmonia heaved herself out of the driver's seat and thumped onto the grass with the reins still in her hand. She looped them through a heavy iron ring bolted to the side of the wagon and tied them off. Familiar with the routine, her mules patiently waited while she set the wagon's chain and shoe brake.

She untied the reins and brought them forward in a sweeping motion. Tossing them on the ground, she began removing the mule's lines, bit and collar. One at a time, she led them into the grazing area, hobbling them so they couldn't wander. "There," she said, dusting her palms one against the other, "that ought to keep you for the night." The caravan's other livestock soon joined hers in the temporary enclosure.

Leaving his second in command to supervise the work of establishing camp, Eumenes and his fellow traders gathered their samples and headed for the city center.

Miryam remained in the shade, watching the men work. She listened to an errant breeze rattle through the branches above her and smiled. The noisy leaves brought to mind David and his men waiting for a similar sign before attacking the Philistines in the Valley of Rephaim.

Splitting into groups, the men worked in unison to raise the tents. One gang set posts and strung lines. As soon as they moved on to the next unit, another man came behind them with an armload of rolled tent fabric. Woven from black goat's hair, the coarse, heavy fabric provided protection from the chilly nights. After he'd formed the roof by laying wide strips from side-to-side across the ropes and hung the side curtains, he returned to the supply wagon for rugs to unroll for the floor.

The young women she'd seen the day she'd booked passage used the opportunity to go down to the creek and bathe. Miryam briefly considered joining them, but decided against it.

The women, not much older than she was, ignored her as they passed. They chattered among themselves as they followed a winding path down to the water. They left their towels on the stony bank and quickly disrobed. Dangling their garments from nearby tree limbs, they stepped into the free flowing stream.

Cool water would feel good after a hot day on the road, Miryam thought, listening to them splash and frolic as they bathed. Their shrieks and laughter echoed around her and throughout the camp.

Detecting movement in her peripheral vision, Miryam turned. She noticed a man crouching in the underbrush near the path leading to the stream. Hidden among the foliage, he watched the young women as they bathed.

Recognizing Cerberus, she called down to them, alerting the women to his presence and pointing to the watcher in the bushes. They merely laughed and turned to raise their arms to the sky, giving him a better look. Shocked, Miryam rose and headed across the compound.

Cheeks still burning, she got into line to eat. The cook had strips of marinated meat sizzling on the grill, fresh bread from the oven, pickled vegetables and salads. The tantalizing aromas made her stomach growl.

"You are not one of the workers," the cook said when she stepped forward to be served.

"No, I am traveling to Nazareth in Galilee and came to get my supper."

"The cost of the evening meal is one *dupondius*. You can come back for seconds if you wish."

"The money I paid Eumenes to travel with his caravan was supposed to include meals."

"Did he tell you that?"

"I never asked. I, I just assumed..."

"Any money you paid Eumenes went into *his* pocket. I have to earn a living too. Those who do not pay do not eat." He motioned her aside. "You are holding up the line. There are others behind you."

Miryam slowly crossed the compound, staring at the grass as she walked. She dug into her sack and pulled out the final loaf Elisheva had given her. Unlike the ones at the cook's tent, hers had begun hardening around the edges. She cracked it in half, putting aside a little bit for breakfast the following morning.

The trip would take five and one half days. One day had already elapsed and she still had a few bites of bread for breakfast. I'll start watching for grain fields as we travel, she thought. I can skim a few handfuls of wheat as we pass and eat it. If that does not work, I will go back to the cook and offer to work for my meal, or perhaps I can buy some leftovers with the few coins I still have in the bottom of my purse. Confident she could survive until she got home, Miryam decided to go to the women's tent and rest.

Sarudi was sitting by the entrance counting his money when she arrived. She slid the strap of her knapsack off her shoulder and, leaning in to the large tent, glanced about.

It surprised her to see tent cloth strung from cross ropes strung between the posts. They divided the interior into a series of small rooms. Each space had a lantern dangling from above and Arabian poufs and a large mattress on the rug. The women's tent on the trip south to Beth HaKerem wasn't nearly as luxurious. Miryam noticed some of the young women she'd seen at the stream in their rooms combing their hair and applying make-up.

A man's deep voice interrupted her inspection. "I am Sarudi. Was there something you wanted?"

"Is this the women's tent?"

"I suppose you could call it that," he said without looking up from his counting.

Miryam smiled. "Should I just pick one of the empty spaces?"

"Why would you want to do that?" Sarudi warily asked.

"Well, I *am* a woman traveling with the caravan, and I need a place to spend the night. So I came to the women's tent."

He ran his eyes up and down her. "No one stays here for free. I can arrange for you to have a spot, if you are willing to work for it," he said with a leering wink.

She didn't understand the meaning of his words at first. And then she did. Miryam's eyes widened. "You mean those women are...are...are," she sputtered, unable to say *the word*.

Sarudi leaned his shoulder against a tent post, crossed his arms, and smiled. "Do not be so quick to judge. You might like it. Go to the cook's tent and tell him you work for me. He will bring you as many glasses of wine as you wish." He grinned, displaying rotted teeth. "Since this is your first night, you will sleep with me. That is how the girls learn."

She turned and ran.

With nowhere else to go, Miryam retreated to her spot under the mulberry trees and nibbled the piece of bread she'd allotted for her evening portion. As the sun sank beneath the horizon and the sky began to darken, she noticed men forming a queue in front of the women's tent. Sarudi sat at the entrance taking their money and assigning them to one of his *girls*. When Miryam could not stand the sight of such debauchery any longer, she wrapped her cloak around her as a bedroll and recited her evening prayers.

The rattling of the mulberry leaves woke her a few hours later. Propping herself up on one elbow, she glanced around. It took her only seconds to identify a heavily intoxicated Cerberus tracing a wobbly path toward her.

She quickly scooped up her belongings and scurried over the hill. Peering between the foliage, she watched him examine the area where she'd been lying.

When he couldn't find her behind the trees, Cerberus staggered down the path. He wobbled from side to side, shoving branches aside. "Mere-Yum, where are you? Mere-Yum where have you gone?" he softly called like someone summoning their pet cat or dog.

Cerberus grew increasingly frustrated when she didn't respond and muttered threats and curses. He stepped into a hole and fell into a patch of thorns. "Where are you," he shouted as he struggled to rise. "You cannot hide forever. I will search you out wherever you are."

Miryam stayed hunkered down in a small cavity behind a bush. Her hands tenderly caressed her abdomen when the infant inside began moving about. "Do not be afraid, little one. I will not let him find us," she whispered.

Without warning, Yosef jerked awake from a sound sleep. He snapped up in his bed, heart pounding and gasping for breath. He pressed the flat of his hand over his heaving chest as his eyes searched the dim room.

The night light still burned in its niche. Everything seemed in place.

Thoughts of Miryam suddenly filled his mind.

Where was she?

Though he had no way of knowing the how and why of it, Yosef was certain she was in great danger. Quaking with fear, he dropped his face into his cupped hands, pleading with God to protect her. Taking several deep gulps of air to calm himself, he spent the rest of the night praying for her safely and well being.

Miryam cautiously inched away from the path Cerberus was on, hoping to circle around behind him and flee into the darkness. A blindingly bright light flashed across the path above as she started to rise. Terrified, she dropped to the ground and curled into a ball, wrapping her arms over her head.

An ominous silence settled over the thicket. Miryam trembled in the dark, afraid to stay, yet afraid to go.

She flinched when she felt a gentle touch on her shoulder. Cautiously peering out between her fingers, Miryam saw Gavri'el beside her. He extended a hand and helped her to her feet.

"I have never been so frightened," she said as she shook out her clothing. "I feared Cerberus would harm us."

"That man will never bother you again," Gavri'el said. He touched her hand. "Have no fear; you are never alone." And then he was gone.

Relying on the glow from the lamps at the Women's Tent, Miryam made her way back to the trees and lay on the ground. Despite the chill in the air, a cocoon of warmth wrapped itself around her. She closed her eyes and fell in to a peaceful slumber.

~ 26 ~

As always, Eumenes planned to wrap-up his transactions, break camp and leave for Shechem by mid-morning. Merchants hurriedly concluded negotiations and delivered merchandise before they left. Roustabouts had already begun striking the tents and the handlers started lining up the camels for loading. Workers and other caravan members formed a long line at the cook tent, anxious to get something to eat before undertaking the day's journey.

The camp was abuzz with all sorts of speculation about what might have happened to Cerberus. Rumors floated in the air as Miryam crossed the compound. One of his tent mates finally resolved the mystery when he stepped forward to announce he'd seen Cerberus frantically packing in the middle of the night. When he asked where he was going in such a hurry, Cerberus whispered, "As far away from here as I can get." He last saw him sprinting down the road, nervously glancing back over his shoulder as he ran.

Miryam inwardly smiled at the news and found a spot to sit and eat her last remaining morsels of bread. A shadow fell across her as she chewed. Lifting her eyes, she saw one of merchants, the woman she'd heard people call Harmonia, standing above her.

"Is that scrap of bread all you have for breakfast?" Harmonia asked in a firm, but non-threatening tone.

Miryam meekly nodded.

"You'll need more than that if you are going to walk all the way to Shechem."

"I have no money," Miryam said. "I did not realize I would be expected to pay for my food when I booked passage."

"It is another of Eumenes' many schemes to wring the last *quadran* out a traveler's purse." Harmonia's eyes narrowed. "I've kept my eye on you ever since we left Jerusalem. You are with child, are you not?"

"Yes, I am," she replied, lowering her eyes.

Resting her hands on her hips, Harmonia addressed the young woman before her like a mother dealing with an obstinate child. "If you do not care about your own needs, think of your unborn child. I want you to get up off the ground and come over to my wagon. We'll be on the road within the hour and you both need more than those few crumbs to sustain you."

She'd already set up a table and two chairs beside her wagon. Harmonia sat in one chair and directed Miryam into the other. She caught the eye of one of the cook's helpers and signaled to him. He appeared a moment later with a platter containing fresh bread still warm from the oven, soft cheese, fruit and honey. Harmonia took the platter from him, placed it in front of Miryam, and sent the young man back for another.

"Where are you headed?" she asked as they ate.

"I am going as far as the Nain," Miryam replied between bites. "My home is in Nazareth. It is only a short distance from there." She hadn't realized how hungry she was. At that moment, the food tasted better than any she'd ever eaten.

"It often gets lonely traveling mile after mile with no one to talk to. Why not ride with me the rest of the way?" Reaching across the table, she patted her hand. "I sense having someone to talk to would benefit us both."

Miryam offered to return the plates and utensils to the cook tent when they finished. While she was gone, Harmonia folded the small table and chairs and stowed them in her wagon.

"Would you like to wash before we leave? It will refresh you for a long day on the road," Harmonia said when Miryam returned.

Memories of Cerberus crouching in the bushes the previous evening caused her to hesitate.

Harmonia read her thoughts. "You need not go to the stream. There is plenty of room inside my wagon."

She gave the wagon's door a push. It swung aside allowing Miryam to see in. Modeled after those the Legions used, the wagon had an oak frame and body with a canvas top stretched over curved staves for a roof. Its interior appeared surprisingly spacious.

Harmonia reached for a bucket dangling on a hook beside the wagon's tailgate. "I will be working right outside. No one will bother you," Harmonia called back to her as she left to draw water.

Miryam examined the wagon's interior as she bathed. It surprised her to find the area so orderly. She'd glanced into some of the other wagons as she went back and forth across the compound. Most of them were a jumble of crates, barrels and parcels stacked to the roof. With little or no space to move about, the owners had to drop the tailgate and shift things around whenever they wanted something.

By comparison, Harmonia's wagon was practically empty. A rolled-up cushion for sleeping stood in one corner beside a closet that Miryam guessed held her clothing. The folded table and a chair rested against one wall. The other chair sat open in the center of the wagon next to the wash bucket. A row of cabinets ran along the opposite wall with a couple of trunks on the floor beneath them.

If she was a merchant, where was her merchandise?

When she finished, Miryam hung her towel to dry. She'd taken a clean homespun tunic, cloak, loincloth and scarf out of her knapsack earlier and laid them over the chair. She pulled the tunic over her head and let it drop around her ankles. Looping a plain girdle made of woven rope around her waist, she knotted it and slipped her feet into her sandals. She reached into her knapsack and extracted an ivory comb.

She hummed to herself as she ran it through her hair. Once the tangles were out, she combed it straight back and gathered it in her left hand. Placing a polished stick between her teeth, she laid a piece of tooled leather over the hank of hair and secured it with the stick. Outside, she could hear the shouts of drovers as the wagons prepared to roll. After dumping the water and returning the bucket to its hook, Miryam walked to the front of the wagon with a smile.

Harmonia had already harnessed her team and waited in the driver's seat for the signal to pull out. There was room enough beside her for a passenger. Putting her foot in the heavy metal loop that served as a step, Miryam grabbed a handle beside the seat and hoisted herself up and in.

When their turn came, Harmonia snapped the reins and urged the mules walk on. After executing a tight turn, they fell into line. The caravan exited the grassy expanse heading north. A short time later they passed Shiloh's ancient city walls, now cracked and tumbled down in places. Looking to her right, Miryam saw smoke rising from a Samaritan shrine on the barren hill which once held the Israelite Tent of Meeting

The *Road of the Patriarchs* bypassed Shiloh and continued on to Shechem. The two women said little to each other during the early part of the trip. Harmonia concentrated on driving the team while Miryam took advantage of the high seat to enjoy the passing scenery.

The wagon had an overhang on the front to protect the driver from sun and weather. They sat side-by-side in its shade, gently swaying in unison as the wagon's steel leaf springs flexed then relaxed with monotonous regularity. Each lost in their own thoughts, they let the rhythmic sway of the wagon lull them into a torpor.

Miryam absentmindedly concentrated on the paving stones as they passed under the wagon's tongue and disappeared beneath them. The constant back and forth traffic of steel-banded wagon wheels had ground the surface as smooth as a marble floor. Their precise grid of squares and rectangles gleamed in the midday sun.

At the day's first rest stop Miryam dipped into a bin at the back of the wagon and scooped oats into the mule's nosebags while Harmonia went for water. Cooperating on these simple tasks helped break down the barriers between them and, for the first time, they enjoyed a friendly chat while sharing a quick midday meal.

Harmonia pointed to a distant mound as they stowed gear and prepared to get underway again. "That is Mt. Gerizim in the distance. We will pass around its east side. Shechem, our next stop, rests in a fertile valley between it and Mt. Ebal. I've heard the people here regard Mt. Gerizim as a sacred place."

Miryam nodded in agreement. "They do. Many years ago the Samaritan people built a temple atop Mt. Gerizim and claimed it, not Jerusalem, was the proper site for worship. This controversy created a rift between the Jews and the Samaritans. John Hyrcanus, a ruler during the resurgence of the Jewish Monarchy, destroyed the temple."

The reins hung lightly between Harmonia's fingers. She glanced over at Miryam beside her. "You seem to know a lot about these things. You must travel this route often."

"I have never been on this road before," she said with a smile. "We Jews avoid the Samaritan territories whenever we can. Had I known you were coming this way, I would not have booked passage with Eumenes."

Harmonia reached out to squeeze her hand. "Well, I am glad you did."

~ **27** ~

The caravan left Shechem early the following day and headed north and west to Sebaste. Known as Samaria for the better part of a millennium, it became the capital of Israel after the division of Solomon's Kingdom. This *watchtower city* sat astride the primary invasion route from the north and endured a long and tragic history of siege and conquest.

The first attack came from the Assyrians. Their king, Shalmaneser, destroyed the Kingdom of Israel, carrying away the ten northern tribes and replacing them with foreigners. Four hundred years later, Alexander the Great again broke down its walls, killing most of the residents. Two hundred and fifty years after that, the Roman General Pompey annexed the region for Rome. Samaria was one of the cities Herod rebuilt and embellished when he became king. He promptly renamed it *Sebaste*, the Greek form of *Augustus*, to honor his patron, Caesar Augustus.

As they traveled Miryam decided to raise a question that had bothered her since she bathed inside Harmonia's wagon. "I was surprised to find your wagon so empty. Most of the merchants have product stacked to the roof."

"I sell jewelry. It does not take up much space. Those two trunks you saw hold all of my merchandise."

A light breeze ruffled Miryam's veil as they descended into the valley. From a distance Sebaste reminded Miryam of Sepphoris, another of the cities which Herod rebuilt in the Roman pattern. "Whatever possessed you to become a traveling merchant?"

"Possessed, indeed. You could not have chosen a more apt word. Everything about my life changed the moment I met Dimitrios." Softly chuckling, Harmonia gave Miryam a sidelong glance and lightly poked her elbow into the young woman's ribs. "Men have a way of doing that to us, do they not?"

"Was he also a merchant?"

Harmonia nodded as she pulled back on the reins and hollered for the mules to stop. "He mostly traveled alone then, sometimes with one or two others. I caught his eye when he came to our village. Or perhaps he caught mine. It makes no difference; we both knew what was in our hearts. After we married I joined him in his wagon. It was just the two of us then," she said, relishing the fond memories.

"We were young and very much in love." Her eyes traced the swelling under Miryam's tunic. "It does not take long when everything is new, does it?"

Miryam's fingers toyed with the corner of her veil. "Yes, suddenly being with child can be quite a surprise." While staying with Elisheva she'd found that omitting certain clarifying details about her situation made social interchange easier.

"Like you, I found I had a new life within me. We returned to our home in Galatia when the trading season ended. The baby came the following spring. Now we were three. Kassandra and I accompanied Dimitrios while he plied his trade."

Their conversation lapsed when, unlike their previous stopovers, they passed through a large gateway with watchtowers on both sides and entered the city of Sebaste. Like all Roman-styled cities, it had a wide boulevard leading to a central Forum. Streets regularly branched off this main thoroughfare at right angles, creating a series of regular blocks on either side.

Miryam surveyed the city as Harmonia guided the wagon to a large undeveloped area set aside for trade caravans. She spotted an amphitheatre, the columns of several temples and administrative buildings over rows of apartment buildings bordering their space.

Due to Sebaste's close proximity to Shechem, they arrived early in the day. The merchants quickly gathered their goods and headed off to the Forum. Their travel schedule called for them to conclude their transactions that afternoon and be ready to leave for Ginae at first light.

Their early morning exit from Sebaste led them through the Jezreel Valley. Several hawks wheeled and soared above the high hills that encircled this wide and agriculturally rich area. It marked the northern border between Samaria and Galilee. Their early start allowed them to reach Ginae, home to the Herodian Estates, before nightfall. A silent sigh of relief escaped Miryam's lips as the wagon rolled to a stop. After 4 days of travel, they were back in Jewish territory.

Taking advantage of the mild weather, Miryam and Harmonia arranged a table and chairs under the overhanging branches of a nearby tree and enjoyed a late dinner. A deep friendship had blossomed between them in a short time and this was their last night together.

"You have been providing my food and transportation," Miryam said. "What can I do to repay you?"

Harmonia took a sip of wine and ran her tongue around the inside of her cheek as she thought. She smiled. "There is one thing you *can* do for me."

"Whatever it is, I will happily do it."

Harmonia removed a small wooden box from deep in her pocket. Keeping it in the shadows, she removed something. "Wear this," she said and placed it in Miryam's palm.

Miryam gasped. Her eyes widened the longer she looked down at the teardrop-shaped gemstone dangling from the fine gold chain that dripped between her fingers. She turned it in the lamplight. Deep blue and finely polished, the stone appeared to have gold dust sprinkled through it.

She began shaking her head. "I cannot take it from you. This necklace is an expensive piece of jewelry. I meant I would be willing to clean your wagon, or wash your clothes, maybe sew a garment for you. I am already in your debt, how could I possibly fulfill that obligation by taking even more from you?"

She tried to return it, but Harmonia refused to take it back. "You are not a slave. I do not want you washing or cleaning or sewing for me. Your presence these last few days has been blessing enough. I ask for nothing more."

Eyes lowered, Miryam cradled the necklace in her lap as she listened to what her benefactor had to say.

"They call the stone *Sapphiros*. They mined it in Ecbatana, the ancient capitol of the Medes and Persians now ruled by the Parthians. I bought it in Egypt a number of years ago. I am told *Sapphiros* was a particular favorite of Queen Cleopatra, the last Egyptian ruler and consort of Marc Antony."

Miryam's face revealed her confusion. "You would have me wear the jewels of an Empress? I have done nothing to merit a gift such as this."

"Hear me out," Harmonia said. "Perhaps you will find it more acceptable after you know the story behind it. I purchased the necklace with someone in mind, my beloved daughter, Kassandra."

"Why is she not wearing it now?"

"She was just a child when I bought it. As soon as I saw it I knew, like my darling Kassandra, it was special. I carried it over my heart until I got home and could put it in a safe place. I was saving it for the future, and planned to give it to her when she conceived her first child."

Tears sparkled in her eyes. Harmonia sobbed. "But it was not to be. The following winter Roman troops brought camp fever to our village. Kassandra fell ill. A few days later she was gone. She was barely three years old. Two weeks later Dimitrios followed her into the next world. In an instant, everything I had, everything I cared for had been ripped away from me."

Her body shook as she wept. Miryam held her tightly, attempting to drive away the demons that tormented her.

After a time Harmonia lifted her head and dried her eyes. "She would be about your age by now," she said with a deep sigh.

Looking away, Miryam watched one of the drovers cross the compound as she listened.

"I am not foolish enough to imagine I can have her back. But being with you these last few days allowed me to pretend that Kassandra was riding beside me. Your thoughts became her thoughts; your child her child."

Harmonia ran her eyes over the young woman beside her. "It pleases me to think Kassandra would be a lot like you. She would have had your beauty and enthusiasm. She would exhibit the same virtues: bravery and determination, grace, humility, modesty, purity, wisdom ...wonder."

She took Miryam's hand in hers. "Indulge a broken-hearted mother by accepting the gift she's longed to give for all these many years. Kassandra is gone. I want you to have the necklace I intended for her. If you think of her each time you wear it, she will not be forgotten."

Harmonia took the necklace out of Miryam's hand. Spreading the chain, she placed it around her neck, smiled, and gently kissed her cheek.

Miryam lifted the pendant and stared at it. "I wish I could have known her," she whispered. "I am terribly sorry for your loss. It must have been unbelievably difficult."

"I had no one. The world looked bleak. What was I to do? Kassandra and Dimitrios were not the only ones in our village. The fever that stole a piece of my heart took away other husbands and fathers as well. Their widows were just as bereft as I was, maybe more so.

"Then an idea came to me. I had dabbled in jewelry when I traveled with Dimitrios. What if I became a merchant? I knew how to manage the wagon; I knew the routes, the process. The widows could craft the items I would sell. Together, we could all survive."

"And you set about establishing a new life," Miryam said.

"It was not easy at first. Most caravans do not want a woman traveling with them. Oh, Sarudi can take along as many of his whores as he likes. The more the merrier, isn't that what they say? But there is no place for an honest woman trying to earn a living."

"Is that why you travel with Eumenes, because he will have you?"

"He tolerates my presence." Harmonia ran her eyes across the tents and wagons around them and sighed. "This caravan is an evil enterprise. Eumenes pretends to have nothing to do with things, but he takes a portion of the money Sarudi's girls bring in. Whenever the mood strikes him, he takes one of them into his tent. They are merely a means to an end, slaves Sarudi exploits for his own purposes. He and Eumenes grow rich, while the girls receive next to nothing."

~ 28 ~

It was still dark outside when Harmonia shook Miryam awake.

"Is something wrong?" she asked, rubbing her eyes and blinking in the light.

"I just received word. The King and his entourage arrived yesterday evening. We are going to the palace. Put on your best clothing. I will style your hair once you have dressed."

Miryam propped herself up on one elbow. "King...what King?"

"King Herod, of course. Is there any other?"

Harmonia knelt on the floor and unlocked one of her trunks. Her fingers quickly danced across the trays of jewelry, picking some out and leaving others. The compartmentalized hinged case she'd opened on the floor gradually filled with necklaces, brooches, earrings and pins.

Rising, she opened a cabinet on the wall and removed several padded boards covered with sumptuous blue and purple fabrics. Perfectly sized to fit into the case, she placed them over the jewelry and latched the lid. Sliding it aside, she opened another just like it and began filling it.

Seeing Miryam still on her sleeping mat, Harmonia paused long enough to wave her arms at her. "Get up! You heard me; we have an appointment with the King," she said and returned to her work.

Miryam stretched and yawned. "I find it hard to believe you really know King Herod."

"Well, seeing is believing. If you are dressed and ready by the time his mercenaries arrive, you can accompany me to the royal estate."

Despite Miryam's protestations, Harmonia insisted on

applying makeup after she dressed. Dipping into her cosmetic case, Harmonia applied color to Miryam's lips and a dusting of rouge on her cheeks. When she pulled out the kohl for her eyes, Miryam refused claiming it was only used by prostitutes. Before she could stop her, the older woman swathed rose scented ointment on her neck.

Herod's men appeared at first light. Tall, brawny and blond, the Germanic troops had the characteristic appearance of the northern tribes in Germania. They were clad in white tunics with Herod's insignia on the upper left arm, plumed helmets, and the standard hobnailed caligea of the Roman army. Each man carried a spear and wore a holstered gladius at his right hip.

Harmonia pointed out the two merchandise cases. Each man grabbed the handle of a case and the four of them headed off.

"This is always the most profitable stop for me," Harmonia said as they walked. "Unlike the shopkeepers who buy my wares for resale, price is not an issue for the King. If he wants it, he buys it."

"Is that why you brought so much?"

"In addition to Herod's family and friends, the wives of his stewards and other officials will also be there." She winked. "Today's sales will determine how well my neighbors and I live this coming winter."

"Just going to the palace does not insure an audience with the King," Miryam said. "Have you ever met him?"

"Yes, a number of times. He has always treated me well. It surprises me to hear he is not well-liked by many of your people."

"It is a complicated issue," Miryam said, trying to avoid controversy.

"The King often purchases something exquisite for his wife, Mariamne."

Miryam's eyes widened. "The Hasmonean princess,

Mariamne, has been dead for almost twenty-five years. Herod was the one who ordered her execution."

"True, but we will not say anything to remind him," Harmonia replied in the tone reserved for motherly commands. "The King, you see, sometimes forgets she is gone."

"At the end of the day he must surely realize his error. What happens to the jewelry he buys for her?"

Harmonia shook her head. "Who knows? Some have whispered that it ends up in her crypt. They say he has surrounded her ossuary with the many jewels he bought while trying to right a wrong that occurred so many years ago. I have also been told he speaks to her as he wanders the halls of the palace late at night."

The sheer size and magnificence of the palace astounded Miryam. The elaborate mansions Yosef described after his trips to Sepphoris couldn't begin to compare to the opulence she encountered as they crossed its antechambers and traversed its corridors and halls.

One of the King's servants led them into a spacious room with thick carpets on the floor and frescoes on the walls. A row of south facing windows overlooked pools, fountains and carefully manicured gardens. Several couches were pushed aside to make room for tables brought in for Harmonia's use.

Miryam distributed the padded display boards across the linen tablecloths while Harmonia followed behind, arranging the various pieces to their best advantage. Everything was in readiness when Harmonia noticed that Miryam had tucked the necklace she gave her into her tunic.

Crossing the room, she pulled the chain out and positioned the pendant in the center of Miryam's chest. "It looks beautiful on you. How can we sell my wares, if you hide them?"

As customers came and went the two women fell into a

comfortable routine. While Harmonia concluded the sale and collected payment, Miryam brought out new items to replace those they'd sold and welcomed newcomers to the tables.

Both of the women were preoccupied with customers when the room suddenly fell silent. Miryam heard the muffled shuffling of feet behind her as everyone vacated the room. The baby unexpectedly kicked. A sense of foreboding sent tingles of apprehension rippling through her.

Keeping her back to the room's entry, Miryam swiped a hand across her abdomen to still the infant within her. She took a deep breath. Consciously willing her body into motion, she slowly turned.

Two men stood in the doorway. She immediately identified the man with white hair and beard as the King. A spider web of tiny veins crisscrossed his cheeks giving the man's ashy skin its only color. Despite the morning warmth, elaborately brocaded robes hung on the man's gaunt frame. Rather than masking the ravages of time, they accentuated it. He relied on the young man beside him for a steadying arm.

About Miryam's age, the smooth cheeked young man wore his short dark hair curled in the Roman style. The neck, short sleeves and hem of his purple tunic were accented with white patterned bands. She had never seen anything like the fabric of the young man's tunic. Thinner than wool or linen, it seemed to glisten in the sunlight and softly rustled as he moved.

Harmonia left her work and rushed to join Miryam. They genuflected together, bowing deeply. "Welcome Herod, King of the Jews, may you enjoy peace and a long life," Harmonia said.

Miryam tried not to stare at the brown age spots spattered across the back of the man's hand when he motioned them to rise.

Approaching Harmonia, Herod took her hands in his and smiled. "It is good to see you again, my dear." He eyes went to the young man at his side. "This is my youngest son, Antipas. I named him after my father." He patted the boy's hand. "It's good to have him back home again. He's been studying in Rome."

Harmonia bowed to Antipas. "It is a privilege to meet the son of the King. I am sure you bring back much knowledge to the kingdom."

Herod ran his eyes around the room. "What have you brought us today?"

"As always, I have saved the best for Herod, my most important client. Come and see for yourself." She led him to a table in the back of the room set apart from the others.

Miryam watched them converse as they walked. It bothered her to see Herod clutching Harmonia's arm as they crossed the room even if he sought stability, not affection.

Turning away, she began re-arranging the items on one of the tables. Her baby suddenly thrashed within her. "It is alright," she said as she worked, "you have nothing to fear."

"Who were you talking to?" a masculine voice asked.

Miryam turned and gasped. She hadn't realized Antipas was so near. "I...I was just thinking out loud. I meant nothing by it."

His brows lowered as he studied her. "Do I frighten you?"

Her heart pounded as her unborn child continued squirming. She swallowed hard and took a breath. "No. I have never been in a King's palace before."

He rested his hand over hers. "You are shaking. Let me help you."

"I will be fine." She pulled away and knelt to sort jewelry. "I do not wish to offend you, but I do not require your help."

He smoothed his tunic and frowned. "I had forgotten how backward the people are here. In Rome a young woman appreciates a man's attention." Antipas walked to a window, crossed his arms and stared out at the gardens.

Meanwhile, on the other the room Herod continued selecting items. Harmonia's mood grew more animated with each successive purchase. He seemed motivated more by her growing delight at the day's sales than any real need on his part. He primarily bought her wares to keep on hand as spur of the moment gifts.

When he had all he wanted, Herod turned and headed in Miryam's direction. "Who is this attractive young woman who accompanied you?" he asked Harmomia as they walked. "A daughter perhaps?"

"She is just a friend who has shared my wagon."

Miryam's stomach roiled as the infant tossed and kicked more than ever before.

Herod smiled when his eyes dropped to Miryam's bosom.

Her cheeks flushed. The physical changes brought on by carrying a baby made her more sensitive to a stranger's gaze.

Without a word, he extended his arm and slipped a finger under the chain of the necklace near her shoulder. Raising his hand, he deftly lifted the teardrop-shaped gemstone. He palmed the stone and bent forward to examine it. "Such a lovely necklace" he said with a sigh. "Every time I see a woman wearing *Sapphiros* I am reminded of my dear departed friend, Cleopatra of Egypt."

He looked up and caught Harmonia's eyes. "Do you have others? Mariamne would love one like it."

Sensing Miryam's growing discomfort, she stepped between them and eased the gem out of his hand. "I have several. Let me get them for you."

Herod purchased a *Sapphiros* necklace for his long dead wife, gathered the other items and left with Antipas.

Harmonia slowed, putting distance between them and the

guards. "What made you so uncomfortable around Herod and Antipas?"

"Did Herod notice?"

"If he had, you would have known. Fortunately, he was not paying attention when you snubbed Antipas."

"Will Antipas say anything?"

Harmonia laughed. "And admit to his father that a Jewish girl with no royal blood and no connections rejected him? But you still haven't told me why you were so uncomfortable."

"I had a bad feeling the entire time Herod and that son of his were in the room," she whispered. "A malevolent presence entered the room with them. They are both evil men."

"You met the King and the son of a King," Harmonia said with a shrug. "Show me one king or prince who is not evil."

"I sensed Herod wanted to harm my baby."

"Such feelings are just maternal jitters." Harmonia shook her head. "What a thought. I am sure you are imagining things."

"The baby felt it too. I could tell."

"Why would Herod care anything about your child? You are just one of many subjects he cares nothing about. Besides, he is an old man. He was probably unaware that you are even with child."

"Perhaps," Miryam said, warily. "Nevertheless, I am glad I will have my baby in Galilee, far away from Herod." An involuntary shiver rippled through her. "Nazareth is a small village. My baby will be safe there. Herod will never find us."

~ 29 ~

"When his mother, Mary, had been betrothed to Joseph, before they came together she was found to be with child..."
~ Matthew 1:18

Harmonia steered the wagon aside at the road to Nazareth and let the caravan pass. She noticed the concern on Miryam's face as the others slowly disappeared from sight and said, "Do not worry. They will stop in Sepphoris. I know the way."

They faced each other, neither wanting to say good-bye yet knowing they must.

"Before you go," Harmonia said, "there is something I must ask. I am surprised your husband allowed you to travel alone in your condition."

"I have been away four months," Miryam said. "When I left, my condition was not known."

She grinned. "I recall how it was when Dimitrios returned from a trip. He will be so surprised when he sees you. I wish I could be there to see his face." She winked. "You two will surely have a celebration tonight."

Miryam bit her lip. "Yes, this evening will be a memorable one. What about you?" she asked, changing the subject. "Where will you go, what will you do?"

"I am on my way home. The mules and I will spend the winter months in silence and peace. Next spring, when the rains end I will load my goods, harness the mules, and set out again to ply my trade." A deep sadness came over her. "People depend on me, you see, and I cannot let them down. In some ways I am just as much a slave as any of Sarudi's girls."

Harmonia tossed her head, shaking off the gloom and grinned. She opened her arms to Miryam. "Next year and all the years thereafter I will carry memories of you with me. Just like Dimitrios and Kassandra, Miryam will always ride beside me as I journey down the dusty roads."

Miryam kept her head down as she walked home. She concentrated on the road and ignored the carts rattling past. Her heart felt like a rock in her chest as she trudged along.

Hiding her condition when Yosef and her parents came for *Shavu'ot* hadn't been a problem since she was not showing much then. She had blossomed in the weeks after they left as the child grew within her. The days of pretending it away were now gone, never to return. One look at her in a tunic was all it would take to reveal her secret.

Yosef will surely understand when I tell him.

She quickly dismissed that silly notion. Only a fool could imagine Yosef, or any other young man, calmly listening while his betrothed attempted to explain the unexplainable. Her appearance alone screamed otherwise. There she would be with a bellyful of baby, getting bigger by the day.

Her mother looked up at the sound of a hand on the latch and smiled when Miryam opened the door. "How was your trip?" Anna asked after they'd hugged.

"Sit down and tell me about it. You must be thirsty; I will fetch you a glass of water."

"It was interesting. The caravan followed the shorter route through Samaria."

"Samaria?" Her mother nearly dropped the glass of water she'd drawn for Miryam. She came out of the kitchen shaking her head. "You traveled through that land of heathens and heretics? I cannot believe my own daughter would do such a thing. Better to travel among gentiles than be in the midst of Samaritans. What will you do next?"

"I had to go where the caravan went. Samaria was nothing like what I expected," Miryam said after draining the glass. "I had little interaction with the people, but they appeared nice enough. The countryside was quite beautiful in places."

"How is Cousin Elisheva?" Anna asked, switching to a safer topic.

"She is doing very well and happy beyond measure. She had a boy. They named him Yohan."

"Yohan?" Anna scrunched up her face as if the word hurt her ears. "There is no one in the family with such a name."

"When the angel Gavri'el visited Zecharias in the Temple of the Lord and told him that Elisheva would conceive and bear a son, he also said they should name him Yohan. Once he did, Zecharias could speak again." Over the next few minutes Miryam told of the angel's prophecy and answered all of her mother's questions.

Anna smiled when Miryam completed her story. "The time of our people's redemption clearly draws nigh. As Zecharias said, the spirit of the Almighty will fill Elisheva's child. He is the one of whom Isaias spoke when he wrote, '...the voice of one crying in the wilderness; Prepare the way of the Lord, make his paths straight.'"

She shook her finger for emphasis. "Your father and I may not live to see the *Mashiach*, but you surely will." Anna closed her eyes and sighed with joy. "Oh, what amazing times we live in. The hand of the Almighty is surely at work all around us."

"What has happened here at home while I was away?"

"Nothing as exciting as the events you experienced in Beth HaKerem."

"How has Yosef been?"

Her mother frowned at the mention of his name. "The man never stops pestering me. Every time I turn around he is there at the door wanting to know if you have returned yet. I know he is lonely without you; we have all missed you, but his constant questioning makes him a nuisance."

Reliving Yosef's obsessive behavior seemed to tire her out. Anna wiped her brow with a cloth. "He will be pleased to see you; more than pleased, elated. Now that you are home perhaps he will leave me alone to do my housework."

She gave her daughter a peculiar look. "Why are you still wearing that dusty traveling cloak?"

"Perhaps Yosef will not be as happy to see me as you imagine." Miryam swept aside the cloak, revealing the small, but undeniable, swelling in her abdomen.

Miryam's revelation seemed to suck the air out of the room.

"You look as if you are with child," Anna said after a long pause. Her incredulous tone begged Miryam to deny it.

Instead her daughter lowered her head and nodded.

"You were always such a dutiful daughter. I never imagined I had to worry about this sort of thing with you." Anna's face unexpectedly brightened. "So you are carrying Yosef's child. Perhaps that is why he wondered when you would return. It is a not a tragedy. You are not the first young woman to succumb to the ardent endearments of her beloved. Your grandmother had an expression for times like this, '*What is...is.*' It is a small setback, but one we can deal with," she said shrugging in resignation.

"Your father will be disappointed of course, but he will get over it. I know how hard it is to say no to a man once you are betrothed." She gave her daughter a knowing wink. "I was young once too, you know. Oh, how your father sulked when I refused him."

Miryam shook her head. "Yosef has never touched me."

"What do you mean, Yosef never touched you?" Anna cried. "Then...then how did this happen?" Anna's eyes widened as the implications became clear. "Another man? And you already betrothed to Yosef? Oh Miryam, how could you do such a thing?"

"I have not betrayed Yosef."

Anna's mind leaped to the only remaining option. "So you were attacked on your way to Beth HaKerem. A woman cannot be blamed for a situation such as this. The brute over-powered you and forced himself on you; you had no choice."

"I was given a choice."

"And this is what you chose?" Anna shrieked. "What about your poor aged parents? Did you even consider that we must now spend our remaining years in a village surrounded by gossip? And then, instead of discussing it with your mother like most girls, you ran away to Beth HaKerem."

"What you say is true, in a way. I left because I wanted, needed, to speak to Cousin Elisheva right away."

Anna's eyes narrowed. "So you are saying this happened while you were with your cousin?"

"No." Miryam gestured toward the doorway leading out to the garden. "It happened right here in our own garden. I was sitting on the patio when the angel Gavri'el came. He told me I would conceive and bear a child whom they would call the Son of the Most High. He is the one who told me Elisheva was with child. That is why I went to see her. If she and Zecharias experienced a miraculous event, I wanted to speak to her about it."

"Yet you did you not feel any need to talk with your own mother about it first?"

Miryam stared at floor. "I feared you would not believe me when I told you," she said in a barely audible whisper.

"But Cousin Elisheva would?"

"Yes. Elisheva understood when I told her my story. She offered the support I needed to understand what was happening to me. Perhaps I should have told you before I left, but I am telling you now. Do you believe me?"

Anna equivocated. "Of course every young woman imagines becoming the mother of the *Mashiach*. But my daughter, and in this strange way?"

"Why was Elisheva chosen to be the mother of his herald? Who can fathom God's mysteries? I want to know if *you* believe me now."

When her mother didn't respond, Miryam knelt and pressed her mother's hands to her lips. "A few moments ago you spoke of the hand of the Almighty at work. You said Yohan will be the *Mashiach's* messenger. How can you believe this for Elisheva, but not for your own daughter?"

Anna pulled her hands away and crossed her arms. Her forehead furrowed. "Well, I believe you are with child. That is a start. As for the rest of what you've told me, we shall see. Fortunately, your father is away for a few days. Maybe we can decide on a course of action before he gets back."

~ 30 ~

"...her husband Joseph, being a just man and unwilling to put her to shame, resolved to divorce her quietly." ~ Matthew 1:19

True to her mother's predictions, Yosef arrived shortly after they'd finished their evening meal.

Anna met him at the door. He read her face and wished he had stayed home. "I can tell Miryam has not returned. I am sorry to have bothered you, Imma Anna," he mumbled and turned to leave.

"Wait, Yosef. Miryam arrived home this afternoon. She is out on the patio. She has been anticipating your visit." Anna picked up a water jug and quickly threw it onto her shoulder. "You two will surely have lots to talk about. I am going to draw some water so you can be alone."

Miryam had her back to the door picking plums when Yosef entered the garden.

"Miryam, you have finally returned. I cannot tell you how much I have missed you." He crossed the patio with a wide smile, opening his arms as he approached her. "I have put our time apart to good use. I worked hard getting the house ready for when you move in after our marriage."

She turned and sat her bowl of plums on the bench.

Yosef gasped. One glance told him all he needed to know. Stunned, he wobbled slightly, grabbed a chair for support then collapsed into it. "I cannot believe what I see. How could you do this to me, to us? Did our marriage contract mean so little that you cast it away without a thought?"

She reached for him with tears in her eyes. "Yosef, this is not what you imagine."

"Imagine? Look at you, Miryam. I imagine nothing." His eyes widened when he took a closer look. "Have you no shame? Did you think I would not notice the expensive necklace you are wearing?"

Miryam quickly scooped up the necklace and slid it into her tunic. "I can explain."

"Explain? Ha! There is no need to hide the necklace now; I have already seen it. Is this why you threw me aside? You have found someone who is wealthy and powerful? An honest carpenter is no longer good enough for you?"

"Do not abandon me now." She stretched her arms out to him. "I need you, Yosef."

He jumped up and stepped away. "You did not need me for," he motioned with a shaky hand, "for, for this." Arms protectively folded across his chest, he glared down at her as she wept. "Do not touch me. The father of your child would not like it."

"Please, Yosef," she begged. "Sit down; at least give me a chance to explain."

"Do you take me for a fool? There is only one explanation and we both know what it is. To even presume you can talk your way out of this is a further insult. There are consequences for actions such as yours. We have the Law to keep order in our society and the Law must be obeyed." Yosef spun on his heel and stormed away without a backward glance.

Yosef staggered out of house, slamming the door behind him. Head bowed and his back bent like a pack animal at the end of a hard day, he blundered his way down the street. He crossed the square dabbing at his eyes.

All of his dreams had turned to ashes in a heartbeat. Over and over again he asked, "Why? What did I do to deserve this?"

When he entered his house, he pushed to door closed and dropped the bar. No matter who knocked, he vowed not to answer it.

What if a friend should call?

He gave a harsh and bitter laugh. He no longer felt like he had any friends. Besides, once the village gossips spread the word about Miryam no one would want to speak to him. He'd become a laughingstock, the butt of everyone's cruel jests.

What if an enemy came to the door?

Enemies? Pah! How could anyone harm him now? He was already as low as a man could go.

What if a customer dropped by?

Let them find another carpenter, he thought, preferably a happily married one. He doubted he would ever set his hands to wood again.

Yosef considered fixing supper, but quickly rejected the idea. The sun slipped below the horizon and heavy clouds blotted out the moon. His humble home grew as dark as his mood, which suited him just fine. He dropped onto the bed knowing he wouldn't sleep.

He tossed and turned in the dark reliving his encounter with Miryam. What should he do? He decided there was only one thing to do. First thing in the morning he would go to the rabbi and make an accusation of adultery against her. One look would confirm his charges.

They will stone her.

A shiver climbed his spine. The idea of consigning her to such a death horrified him. No, he thought, there has to be another way...and he'd find it.

The house became unnaturally quiet. He ran his hands up and down his arms, trying to settle his prickly skin. The flame on the night light quivered then went out. Yosef felt as if he were being suffocated.

He suddenly became aware of another entity there beside him in the dark, an incorporeal presence he couldn't identify. His eyes jerked about, searching the gloom for the source of this phenomenon. He tried to think, but found it impossible to gather his thoughts.

Suddenly another voice, one he didn't recognize, appeared inside his head. Raspy and angry, it diverted his thoughts. The strange presence berated him for his cowardice and urged him to seek revenge.

"Right is right. She made a fool of you in front of the whole town. There is no mercy for women like her. You know as well as anyone the Torah says, 'If a man commits adultery with the wife of his neighbor, both the adulterer and the adulteress shall surely be put to death.' Go to the rabbi. Have her stoned along with that bastard child she is carrying. If you are the God-fearing man you claim to be, you will do what the Law demands."

With great effort, Yosef curled his fingers into a fist and slammed it down on the mattress. "I will not see her stoned!" he shouted.

Whatever, or whoever, invaded his mind immediately vanished. Sweat poured from his body as he lay on the bed panting like a runner at the end of the race.

He started over again, reviewing the situation one step at a time. True enough, the law demanded she be stoned. And, since he was the one she wronged, they would expect him to cast the first stone. He imagined Miryam's broken and bloodied body lying in a ravine. He saw the sadness in Anna and Yoachim's eyes when they turned and looked at him.

The mere thought of it caused him to sob uncontrollably. He raised his arm, wiping his eyes on his sleeve. A part of him wanted to hate her for what she did, but no matter how hard he tried he could not do it.

What if I simply put her away?

Of course, why did he not think of that in the beginning? He could write a bill of divorce. Dissolve the marriage contract. He could send her away without anyone knowing why. Let her go live with her Cousin Elisheva. After all, she had to have known. Or, or let her marry the father of her child. If he rejected her, perhaps she could live as a spinster supporting herself and the child by doing sewing or cleaning a rich man's house. She might have to glean the fields at harvest time to get enough to eat, but anything was better than throwing rocks at her.

He took a deep breath and sighed with satisfaction. It felt good to have finally resolved things. Time for sleep; tomorrow would be a decisive day. He rolled onto his side, closed his eyes and fell asleep right away.

~ 31 ~

"Joseph, son of David, do not fear to take Mary your wife, for that which is conceived in her is of the Holy Spirit; she will bear a son, and you shall call his name Jesus, for he will save his people from their sins." ~ Matthew 1:20-21

The room suddenly became as bright as the sun.

Yosef snapped up in the bed and glanced around. His jaw dropped when he saw the large, man-like creature in the midst of a cloud of shimmering light. He slipped out of his bed and hunched down between the bed and the wall. He grasped the corner of the cloak he'd tossed aside when he lay down and covered his head. Huddling beneath it, he quaked in terror.

, A flick of strange visitor's hand sent the cloak flying across the room.

Yosef opened his mouth to protest and found that fright had stolen his voice. He peeked over the mattress. Wide-eyed and trembling, he stared in mute silence.

The impressive creature's deep voice filled the small room like the rumble of distant thunder. "I am Gavri'el, who stands in the presence of the Eternal God." He motioned for him to come forward. "There are things you must see."

Heart pounding, Yosef inched around foot of the bed. His shaky legs refused to support him as he approached the angel. He pitched forward and would have fallen had Gavri'el not caught him. Yosef grabbed his staff from beside the bed to steady himself.

"This way," the angel said. Clutching him by the arm, he dragged him toward the wall.

Yosef fought against it, but the Gavri'el's grip was unbreakable. Fearing certain death as they neared the brick wall, he threw the staff aside and squeezed his eyes tight shut. An instant later he found himself standing outside his small house none the worse for wear.

One moment he was moving his feet around on the ground, testing its solidity. The next instant everything he knew disappeared in a whirlwind of light and motion.

He opened his eyes and glanced around as his vision cleared. Gavri'el had taken him into the desert. They were on a bare patch of sandy soil surrounded by tents of all sizes. Yosef's eyes moved across the large enclosure in front of him. Bounded by a series of pillars, it had cloth strung between them. People went about their business, going back and forth as if he and the angel were not there.

Looking to his left, Yosef noticed smoke rising from an altar near the front of the enclosure. A soft breeze, thick with the scent of incense, ruffled his hair as it blew by. Searching for its origin, he noticed a goat's hair tent near the back of the enclosure. Despite never having been there before, something deep inside him intuitively responded to what the angel was showing him. He recognized this place.

No, it could not be.

"Tell me, Son of Adam, what do you see?"

Yosef gave a start. He'd become so mesmerized by his surroundings that he'd forgotten about the angel beside him. He swallowed hard and licked his lips. "I, I see the Israelites' encampment in the desert." He pointed across the compound. "With, with the Brazen Altar of Sacrifice and the *Miskan*, the Tabernacle of the Lord in a tent."

"You have spoken well."

In a blink of an eye they were inside the goat hair tent. How they got there, Yosef didn't dare ask. Seven flames burned on a golden lampstand, illuminating the small enclosure. Opposite the lampstand there was a table overlaid with gold. Wine and twelve loaves sat on the table.

Incense burned beside him. Its smoke slowly coiled in lazy

circles as it rose. It accumulated at the ceiling before seeping out and infusing the entire area with its fragrance.

"Tell me, Son of Adam, what do you see now?"

"I see the Menorah and the *Lechem HaPanim*, the Bread of the Presence, and the Altar of Incense. We are in the Holy Place, the Court of the Tabernacle." Stark fear shot through him like a lightning bolt as the reality of where they were sank in. Yosef began to tremble. "I should not be here."

Ignoring his sudden reticence, the angel directed his attention to a veiled entrance. "And what lies beyond the veil?"

The angel's continued grilling left Yosef in a panic. "You know as well as I," he shouted. "The *Qodesh HaQadashim*, the Holy of Holies, lies beyond that veil. Why have you brought me here?"

"So you may enter."

Yosef's arm quaked when he pointed across the small enclosure. "No, no, no! I can never go in there. If I did, I would surely die. *HaShem* has commanded it. To enter the Holy of Holies would defile the dwelling place of the Lord." Fearing the angel might force him across the threshold against his will, Yosef tried to wrench free of his iron grasp.

He was still trying to get away from the angel when the vision of ancient Israel vanished as quickly as it had appeared. Yosef shook his head, blinked, and glanced around. They were back in Nazareth again, but now he was alone.

He heard voices. Curiosity led him to follow the sound, searching for its source. He inched his way along until he ended up outside Yoachim's patio. Finding the gate ajar, he tiptoed closer. Peering through the narrow gap, he watched Gavri'el, the one who had taken him to the Israelite encampment, speaking with Miryam, his betrothed.

Miryam didn't seem to fear Gavri'el the way he had. Her face had an indescribable radiance as they conversed. She had never looked more beautiful. He felt as if his heart might burst.

Then Yosef noticed something else. The fig trees around the patio had no leaves on them. The Israelites had wandered the desert more than a thousand years earlier, yet Gavri'el had taken him to their encampment. Likewise, the events he was now witnessing must have happened months ago, before Miryam left for Beth HaKerem.

Creeping forward, he listened with rising interest. He detected a surprising tenderness in Gavri'el's voice. "Do not be afraid, Miryam. For you have found favor with God. And behold, you will conceive in your womb and bear a son. He will be great, and will be called the Son of the Most High; and the Lord God will give to him the throne of his father David. He will reign over the house of Jacob for ever; and of his kingdom there will be no end."

Yosef read the confusion on Miryam's face when she looked up at Gavri'el. "How shall this be, since Yosef and I have not yet consummated our marriage?"

"The Holy Spirit will come upon you. And the power of the Most High will overshadow you; therefore the child to be born will be called holy, the Son of God. For with God nothing will be impossible."

Miryam stared at the bench, twisting her hands in her lap as she thought.

The angel said no more; he simply waited.

He's awaiting her decision, Yosef realized. A decision she clearly agonized over. It pained him to see her struggle like this. She should not have to face this alone. He wanted to run to her, take her in his arms, and assure her he would always be there to help her. No matter what, he would somehow make everything alright.

He bit his lip and stared at his feet. He'd never felt such overwhelming shame. That was not what he had done when he had the chance. When Miryam begged him to listen, he turned his back on her. Instead of making things easier for her, he made them harder.

He looked around. Time itself seemed to pause as the universe awaited her answer.

Finally, Miryam sucked in a deep breath, lifted her head and threw her shoulders back. "Behold, I am the handmaid of the Lord; let it be done to me according to your word."

And the angel left her.

"Do you understand what you have been shown, Son of Adam?" a deep voice asked from behind him.

Gavri'el was back.

Yosef spun to face him. "Yes, I believe I do."

Gavri'el no longer seemed quite as intimidating as he once had. He rested a friendly hand on Yosef's shoulder. Speaking softly but firmly, he said, "You shall be as Abinadab's son, Eleazar, who was consecrated to keep and protect the Ark of the Lord. Likewise, you must be prepared to act as David did when he safeguarded the Ark from Absalom by fleeing with it."

Though the angel's words confused him, Yosef nodded.

Gavri'el extended both arms and grasped Yosef by the shoulders. For the first time, he appeared to smile. "Yosef, son of David, do not fear to take Miryam as your wife, for that which is conceived in her is of the Holy Spirit; she will bear a son, and you shall call his name Yeshua, for he will save his people from their sins."

~ 32 ~

"When Joseph woke from sleep, he did as the angel of the Lord commanded him; he took his wife, but knew her not..."
~ Matthew 1:24-25

A rooster crowed in the yard beside the window.

Yosef's eyes snapped open. The events of the previous night left him feeling unsettled. He rolled onto his side and glanced around the room. Nothing out of place; everything appeared the same as usual.

He swung his feet over the edge of the bed and sat up. Yosef thumped his feet on the floor several times, reveling in its feeling of solidity. He shook his head to clear the cobwebs. Stroking his beard, he relived his strange dream.

He was prepared to dismiss it as so much nonsense and get on with his day when Gavri'el's parting words resounded in his memory. *"Yosef, son of David, do not fear to take Miryam as your wife, for that which is conceived in her is of the Holy Spirit; she will bear a son, and you shall call his name Yeshua, for he will save his people from their sins."*

Something pulled his eyes over to the far wall, showing him what he'd overlooked while lying in bed. He couldn't miss the staff lying beside the wall where he'd dropped it the night before.

After breakfast Miryam took her sewing basket to a secluded spot on the west side of the house. The weathered plank fence afforded her the privacy she longed for. An ancient fig tree grew in the center of the stone patio. The gnarled tree had long since outlived any commercial usefulness, but it held so many family memories that cutting it down would have seemed sacrilegious.

She arranged her materials on the curved stone bench with a sigh and patted the tree's smooth white bark before sitting down. Miryam recalled kneeling on the patio's flat stones as a youngster and walking her dolls along the bench while her mother shelled peas for their evening meal. Small birds flitted from branch to branch above her, serenading her as she arranged the cloth in her lap and made the first tentative stitches.

After several minutes work she held the piece at arm's length and shook her head. Everyone commented on the evenness of her stitches each time she sewed with the other women. Now, try as she might, she couldn't steady her hand. Her stitches fluttered across the cloth like a flock of frightened chickens.

What was to become of her? Miryam wondered, as she began tearing out the work to begin anew. The tunics she had were becoming too tight to wear. One way or another she had to have larger ones. Morbid thoughts crept into her mind. If Yosef acted on his threats of the previous day, instead of new tunics she would need a shroud.

Miryam instinctively folded her arms across her abdomen at the sound of approaching footsteps. A moment later Yosef emerged from the shadows walking toward her. The baby within her began to stir as Yosef drew closer. He kept his head down, avoiding her eyes as he crossed the flagstone patio.

He came to a stop a few feet in front of her.

"Yosef," Miryam softly said.

Without warning, he dropped to his knees on the hard stones and rested his forehead on her knee. His shoulders quivered as he wept. Tears glistened on his cheeks when he raised his head and looked up at her.

"Yesterday I accused you of betraying me, when in fact it is I who betrayed you. At the moment you needed me the most rather than help I pushed you away, shut my ears and refused to listen."

Her brow furrowed. "What happened to make you change your mind?"

"The angel did."

"The angel? I do not know what you mean."

"Gavri'el. He showed me things, helped me understand, put everything in its proper perspective. I have been given a part in the greatest of events...we both have." He gave her a rueful look. "The difference is you accepted yours with trust and I, well let's just say I required a little nudge. But all that is behind us now. Can you ever forgive me?"

"Get off your knees and come sit on the bench beside me." There was an undertone of wariness in her voice.

Unsure how to gauge her reaction, Yosef slowly rose from the flagstone patio and plopped down on the bench. He left a wide gap between them. Exchanging nervous sidelong glances, the two of them sat there in silence. Miryam passed the time by folding and refolding her cloth. When she was satisfied with the corners, she began re-arranging and tidying her sewing basket. Meanwhile, Yosef dusted his knees and picked imaginary lint from his cloak.

Pretending to examine a berry bush near the fence, Miryam said, "You could move a little closer. That is, unless doing so would make you uncomfortable."

He slid a wee bit closer.

"Would it help if I promised not to bite you?"

Yosef wiggled over a little more then looked away, concentrating on a bee moving among the flowers.

Scooting over beside him, she leaned against him. "Put your arm around me, Yosef. I need to feel you there beside me."

He felt her quivering and held her tighter. "You are shaking; are you cold?"

Miryam shook her head. "Not cold, worried...and frightened if I am honest. Things are happening too fast. I hardly slept at all last night." She glanced up at him. "What is to become of me, Yosef?"

He lifted her chin and kissed her. "Never allow fear to beset you. I will protect you no matter what. You are my wife."

"Some wife I am," she said, pressing her fingers against her temple. "It seems the only dowry I bring is trouble."

"I know a way to put an end to those troubles here and now. The length of the betrothal provides a young man time enough to establish a home for his bride. There is no need for us to wait. I already have a home and a business. We can be married as soon as your father returns from his trip."

She fidgeted on the bench. "Have you forgotten that I am with child?"

He shook his head and repeated Gavri'el's words to her. "This child of yours is of the Holy Spirit. He will be great, and called the Son of the Most High. The Lord God will give to him the throne of his father David and he will reign over the house of Jacob forever; and to his kingdom there will be no end. You shall become my wife, Miryam. I will be his father, and he shall be my son."

"What will people think?"

"Unless we tell them differently, they will assume the child is mine. We both know an *early wedding* is hardly an unknown occurrence. This way we can put an end to the gossip before it starts."

"That is very kind of you." Color rose in her cheeks as she thought about what he'd said. Lowering her eyes, Miryam whispered, "You have to know that should we wed I still...you must..." She took a deep breath, swallowed hard, and said, "Yosef, even after our wedding we could not..."

His finger on her lips stopped her. He smiled down at her and slowly shook his head. "Do not worry about these things. Gavri'el made certain I understood my role in your life. Other than 'Yes,' there is nothing more you need to say."

~ 33 ~

"Behold, I will send you Elijah the prophet before the coming of the great and dreadful day of the Lord" ~ Malachi 4:1-5

Yoachim returned to Nazareth mid-afternoon the following day. Anna gave him time to change and rest before bringing him up-to -date on Miryam's situation and relaying Yosef's request that they hold the wedding ceremony immediately.

Yosef joined them for the evening meal. After the prayer, dishes of food circled the table in silence. Father, mother, daughter and son-in-law all kept their eyes on their plate as they ate. Each of them concentrated on their food, speaking only if spoken to and looking up only when asking for the salt or more water.

As when Yosef came to ask for Miryam's hand in marriage, she and her mother quickly cleared the table after the meal and retreated to the backyard so the men could talk.

Yosef sat ramrod straight, eyes straight ahead. He steeled himself for a rebuke as he waited for Yoachim to speak. Given Miryam's condition, he expected her father to be angry.

The gray haired man took a seat across from him. He leaned to one side and cocked his head. Resting his elbow on the arm of the chair, he laid his left arm across his body to hold his dangling wrist. "I encountered some startling information when I returned home today." He chuckled. "Who knows what might have happened had I been away the entire week."

A fleeting smile crossed Yosef's lips. He quickly suppressed it.

"Miryam and I barely spoke. She seemed more comfortable avoiding me. Anna, however, tells me you wish to wed right away. Is this truly what you want?"

"It is," Yosef said, and started into his carefully constructed and well rehearsed speech.

To his surprise, Yoachim silenced him. "Let me begin by

saying that her mother has already shared with me all the things Miryam told her when she returned from Beth HaKerem."

Yosef took this as his opportunity to once again focus all the blame on himself rather than Miryam, but his father-in-law raised a hand.

"Explanations are unnecessary," Yoachim said. "Indulge an old man by taking the time to first listen to what I have to say. After hearing what my Anna said, I spent my afternoon meditating on the *Nevim*, the writings of the prophets."

He leaned forward, staring intently into Yosef's eyes. "What are we to make of Elisheva? A woman who is old and barren suddenly conceives and brings forth a son? It takes one's mind back to our father, Abraham, and Sarah, does it not?" He gave a low whistle. "And what are we to think about the prophecies the angel made to Zecharias in the Temple?"

"Did you reach a conclusion about these things?"

"I did," Yoachim replied with a confident nod. "For some reason, I thought first about the Prophet Malachi. He wrote, 'Behold, I will send you Elijah the prophet before the coming of the great and dreadful day of the Lord.' Because of this, many have taught that before the *Mashiach* comes, he will be preceded by Elijah returning in a fiery chariot."

"I detect a hint of skepticism in your voice."

"Indeed you do. For a moment suppose, just suppose, that instead of Elijah we should be expecting an individual who acts in the *Spirit of Elijah*. Though not the prophet Elijah, such a man would be a herald, a forerunner, if you will."

Yosef's eyes lit up as he tried the idea on for size. "What an original thought."

"Before you credit me with great insight, I confess to already knowing this is what Elisheva told Miryam the angel said. *In the Spirit of Elijah*, this infant of hers will be, as Isaias said, 'The voice crying: In the wilderness prepare the way of the LORD, make straight in the desert a highway for our God.'"

"He will lead people to the *Mashiach*."

"He will indeed. I understand what you are doing, and respect you for it. You are a good man, Yosef. The Lord chose well when he selected you to be a husband for our Miryam. The two of you have been called to the service of God. Like the prophets of old, your life will not be an easy one, but the rewards awaiting you will be great."

"Then you have no objection to us having the wedding right away?"

"Of course not. It is all preordained." Yoachim's eyes twinkled as he laughed. "While considering Isaias, I was reminded of another of his writings, 'The Lord himself will give you a sign. Behold, a virgin shall conceive and bear a son...' No doubt the Kingdom of God is about to come upon us. Just as Elsiheva did not climb to the rooftop to proclaim the tasks assigned to her son, we too must remain circumspect."

"All will be as God willed it. For everything there is a season, and a time for every matter under heaven," Yosef said.

"Right, and now it is time to let the women start planning this wedding of yours." They rose together and the old man clapped Yosef on the back. "They do enjoy it so."

Anna pulled Miryam's hair back and tied it with the traditional blue ribbon. Taking the flowers she'd cut earlier, she moved behind her daughter weaving them into her dark tresses. Satisfied, she unfolded a lace veil and draped it over her daughter's head. "I wore this veil on the day your father and I were wed," Anna said.

She stepped back to admire her handiwork.

"You look so beautiful." Anna brushed aside a tear and straightened the shoulder seam of Miryam's cloak, adjusting its drape. "There," she said with a note of satisfaction, "everything is perfect. "The fullness of the cut covers your little bulge. Hold your bouquet so the flowering vines trail down." She gave her a conspiratorial wink. "That way, no one will ever know."

"This may work for today, but it will not take people very long to unravel our secret, Imma."

Anna scoffed. "Let them think what they will. No one will utter a word. Do not forget, you will be a married woman by then. And we both know what married women do." Leaning close, she whispered in her daughter's ear, "They have babies."

~ 34 ~

"And it came to pass, that in those days there went out a decree from Caesar Augustus, that the whole world should be enrolled...And Joseph also went up from Galilee, out of the city of Nazareth into Judea, to the city of David, which is called Bethlehem: because he was of the house and family of David, to be enrolled with Mary his espoused wife, who was with child.

~ Luke 2:1-7

Yosef came into the house muttering under his breath and slammed the door shut behind him.

Miryam rushed out of the kitchen, eyes wide and face pale. She tucked her towel into her apron strings with one hand and placed the other over her pounding heart. She let out a long sigh of relief when she saw him.

"Oh, it is you. It sounded like one of the walls fell in. I had to come and see what happened." She nervously moved about the room, straightening things on the table and tidying shelves.

She ran to him when she noticed the bulging veins in Yosef's temple and his flushed face. "What has upset you so, my husband? This is not like you."

He sat down at the table and stared at the wall, brooding. His big hands automatically curled into fists as he thought.

Miryam was beside him in a flash. She put her hand on his shoulder. "Tell me what it is that caused this," she said while rubbing the knotted muscles in his shoulder.

"Who does that man think he is?" Yosef shouted.

She instinctively ran her eyes around the room. "Man, what man?"

"Caesar."

"You are angry at Caesar?"

"Everyone is. If I could, I would place my hands around his

neck and squeeze until his eyeballs popped out," he growled. "One petty tyrant in Rome has the whole world under his thumb. He taxes our animals, he taxes our crops, he taxes the items I buy and he taxes the products I sell. I pay tolls every time I go to Sepphoris and I have to pay again just to come back home to my wife." The table jumped when he slammed his fist down. "He takes and takes and takes until there is nothing left, and yet he still wants more!"

Miryam poured water and forced the cup into his hands despite his objections. "Here, drink something. It will make you feel better. What do you mean, he wants more?"

Ignoring her question, Yosef continued his tirade against Caesar. "Does he care that my wife is with child? No! How am I supposed to live if I have to shutter my business and run off to Bethlehem? Does he care if I lose my customers? No!"

She wrapped her hands around one of his and pressed it to her lips. "You are frightening me, husband. What is all this talk about taxes and closing your shop?"

Her words reached him for the first time. He threw his arm around her and hugged her to his chest. "I never meant to worry you," he said, and gently kissed the top of her head. "A Roman Centurion came into town a short while ago and posted a notice. Caesar has called for a census. Everyone has to stop whatever they are doing and return to our ancestral home to register. He is turning the country upside down."

Miryam thought about what he'd said. Crossing her arms, she gave him a smug smile. "This is no accident. Imagine how many road tolls his soldiers will collect with all those people going back and forth."

The trip to Bethlehem was straight forward enough; they'd done it at least three times every year when they went to Jerusalem for the Pilgrim Festivals. Yosef worked late into the evening to complete all of his open orders before they left. While in Sepphoris he notified his customers there that he'd be away for a time due to the census. They understood, even commiserated, since the machinations of Rome also affected them.

Yosef began packing his tools the day before they left. When Miryam asked about it, he explained that he could take on some small jobs if he had his tools available.

"How will the poor donkey manage the tools with me on his back?" she asked as he was locking up the shop.

He heaved the two leather satchels onto his back and ran straps over his shoulders and crossed them over his chest to hold them in place. "The donkey will not be carrying them, I will," he said with a wry look.

He boosted her onto the donkey's back and they set off, joining others heading the same way. An Emperor on the other side of the Mediterranean had forced this trip upon them. Unlike the times when they traveled to Jerusalem to celebrate, they did not sing Psalms as they walked or share idle chit-chat. No one in the party said much of anything. The men kept their heads down, grumbling to themselves as they slogged along.

The nearness of her due date combined with the heat and constant rocking and jostling of the trip, made it difficult for Miryam to interpret her body's signs. She'd been having occasional contractions for several days prior to leaving. Irregular at first, they came and went without any follow-up. The afternoon and evening of the previous day she experienced several episodes of recurring contractions lasting an hour or more. The midwife in Nazareth warned her about such occurrences, calling them *false labor*. Though uncomfortable at times, Miryam wasn't unduly concerned.

She attempted to describe the situation to Yosef as best she could over supper. Since child-bearing was a new experience for them both, he deferred to her judgment. He scheduled more frequent rest breaks the next day as a precaution. Waking the following morning feeling refreshed and energized, she insisted on ordering and repacking their baggage before they started off.

Because Miryam had no discomfort or signs of impending

delivery, they decided to go straight through to Bethlehem. The sun was setting by the time they passed Jerusalem. Eager to reach their destination and secure lodging, Yosef pushed on. Miryam, too tired to argue at that point, grimly clutched the donkey's girth strap with one hand and kept the other arm folded across her stomach. Widely spaced, but regular waves of pain gripped her abdomen.

Yosef shouted out the good news when he saw lights in the distance. The thought of being so close to their destination gave him a burst of enthusiasm. He smiled when they arrived at the Bethlehem turn off. "Almost there," he whispered under his breath. He'd been repeating this refrain more for himself than Miryam throughout the latter portion of their trip. After several days of '*Almost theres,*' she could no longer stand hearing it and complained. Yosef responded by thinking it rather than saying the phrase aloud.

They headed east on the narrow road leading to Bethlehem. The moon was still low in the sky, casting more shadows than light on the road. Nevertheless, Yosef continued on, guided as much by memory as by sight. Having grown up here, he knew every twist, turn and rocky place along their route.

Yosef led the donkey into the small hamlet, heading for Tovit's house. "I know you are uncomfortable," he said to Miryam as he walked. "We will stop at my brother's home. He will surely make a place for us."

Galena answered the door when Yosef knocked. "Yosef it is so good to see you." She hugged Yosef, then stepped past him and threw her arms around Miryam. "And you as well, Miryam."

They both thanked her for the welcome.

"Tovit just stepped out, but he will return very soon." She took a step back and ran her eyes over Miryam. "I did not realize you were with child when you visited us during *Shavu'ot.* You look as though you are ready to deliver any day."

Her lips formed a tight line. Leaning close, she lowered her voice. "I must warn you, Tovit may not be as pleased to see you. His business has turned sour since you left."

"Then it is good that I brought my tools with me. I will be able to help."

Galena's brow furrowed. "Why would you bring tools to register for the census?"

"As you said Miryam is close to delivering her child. Rather than register and travel right back to the Galilee, we felt it better for her to have the child here. This trip has been hard enough on us both. Once the child is born, she must make the offering of purification 40 days after the birth. It is easier to stay here for six weeks instead of making the trips back and forth."

Galena shocked them both when she glanced over at Miryam and frowned. "All men are alike, are they not? Here you are with your first child and your husband has already decided it will be a boy."

Miryam recovered first and took Galena's hand. "We shall wait and see what the Lord has in store us."

Her sister-in-law smiled in approval. "Where are you staying?" The words were no sooner out of Galena's mouth than she realized this was the reason for their visit. She tapped the side of her head and rolled her eyes. "How silly of me, that is why you stopped."

Stepping closer, she rested an arm on Yosef's shoulder and looped the other around Miryam. "Please do not misunderstand what I am about to say. Your offer of help is a kind one. However, Tovit may not see it that way. Yosef, you know he is a proud man and pride often leads to bitterness. Try to secure lodging with one of your sisters. Better Tovit adjust to the idea of you being back before offering help."

"Suppose neither of them can take us in, what then?" Yosef asked.

Galena caught his eye and winked. "As your wife said, 'Let us see what the Lord has in store for you.'"

~ 35 ~

"And while they were there, the time came for her to be delivered. And she gave birth to her first-born son and wrapped him in swaddling cloths, and laid him in a manger, because there was no place for them..." ~ Luke 2:6-7

Neither of Yosef's sisters could offer them lodging. "Some husband I am," he muttered when he returned to Miryam empty-handed. He picked up the donkey's rein and urged the tired animal on.

He talked as he trod the streets of his childhood. "So what if my family refuses to help us? I do not need family; I have friends in Bethlehem. I will go to them. They will offer us a place to stay." For Miryam's sake he tried to project an optimism which neither of them possessed at that moment.

They'd gone only a short distance when Miryam asked him to stop. Hearing the desperation in her voice, he rushed to her side. "I am here, my wife. What do you need?"

"Lead the donkey into the alleyway where it is dark so I may dismount. Please hurry."

He did as she asked, even though her actions puzzled him. "The blanket across the donkey's back has a damp spot," Yosef said as he set her on her feet.

"Yes, and I am damp as well. It appears one of us has sprung a leak," she said, trying to make light of the situation.

He quietly awaited her explanation.

Miryam sighed "It is a womanly thing. Forgive my attempt at humor. If I do not laugh, I will surely cry."

Yosef looked more confused than ever. Over the last few months he'd learned more about *womanly things* than he ever wanted to know.

She reached into one of the saddlebags and removed a towel. "Turn aside, please."

He turned his back to her. "What has happened that requires a towel?"

"My bag of waters has broken. The baby is coming. I am placing the towel around myself to absorb the flow until we find a place to stay."

He waited in the shadows until she asked him to help her back onto the donkey. He walked around and grasped her under the arms, preparing to lift her onto the animal's back. He paused a moment and stared down at her in the moonlight. He tried to speak, but the words caught in his throat. Bowing his head, he mumbled apologies.

Yosef stopped trying to speak when Miryam slipped her arms around his shoulders. After tenderly kissing him, she gave him a weary smile and shook her head. "None of it is your fault, my husband. You have done your best in a bad situation." Her eyes swept over the darkened buildings with shuttered windows surrounding them. "I would never blame you for any of this, not in a thousand years. There is no need for worry. God will take care of us in His own way and in His own time."

"It hurts me to see you suffer. I so wish I could make things better for you."

"I love you too," she said and patted his hand. "Now help me back onto the donkey before I have another pain."

Yosef noticed a clump of grass growing in the alley when he leaned to grab the reins. He stooped and picked the grass. Waving it in front of the donkey, he enticed him to go on just a little longer.

Much to Yosef's dismay, his friends were of no more help than his relatives. Having run out of options, he headed back to his brother's house.

"Galena said you were here an hour ago. Why have you come back?" Tovit asked.

"I cannot find a place for us to stay." Yosef cupped his hands together as a beggar might. "Tovit, I am begging you to help us."

"I just told you the house is full up, we have no room."

"My wife is about to deliver her child and I have nowhere for her to even lie down."

"Our sister, Moriah, has a large house in Jerusalem. Go see her. She will feel sorry for her little brother and take you in."

"Jerusalem is too far away. Miryam cannot make the trip. How can you treat your own family in such a manner?"

Tovit scowled. "What do you expect me to do? I cannot build another room onto the house while you wait."

"You did not want me to leave. I went anyway and you were angry. Fine. Hate me if you like, but do not punish my wife for what I did. She has done nothing to merit your ire."

Tovit folded his arms over his chest. "So you would like me to put someone else out on the street so you can take their space, hmm?"

Yosef glanced back at Miryam waiting on the donkey. "She is with child, Tovit."

He shrugged his shoulders and showed Yosef his empty palms. "If I had known you were coming, perhaps I could have saved some space."

"Known I was coming?" Yosef's voice grew shriller with each word that came out of his mouth. "You did not know I was coming? Look around you, man. Half the world has come to Bethlehem. Do you think that because I moved to Nazareth I no longer belong to this family? It is not as if I had a choice in the matter. When Caesar says, 'Go home,' I must go home."

"I am sorry you have this problem, but you will just have to find someplace else." Tovit began to close the door in his face.

Yosef thrust his arm out, halting the door's progress. "So what do you suggest? Would you have us go to one of those filthy Roman inns? Perhaps I can convince a whore there to give us her bed for the night."

Galena came to the door carrying a lamp. "Tovit, you will wake up the neighbors. What is all this shouting about? Who is out here at this time of the night?"

When her husband didn't answer, she jammed her elbow in his ribs and shoved past him. She took a step forward and extended her lamp. "Yosef?"

She frowned at the two men like a mother chastising her naughty children. "Brothers should not scream at each other like this. Your blood runs in his veins and his in yours. What would your dear departed father say," she dipped her head in respect, "may he rest in Avraham's bosom, if he saw the two of you fighting?"

"He brought these troubles upon himself. This problem would not exist if Yosef had stayed in Bethlehem where he belonged. You take care of it, if you think you can." Tovit shook his head and went back into the house. "I am going to bed."

Galena touched Yosef's arm. "Why have you come back?"

"My wife is laboring to deliver her first child and I have nowhere else to take her."

The color drained from Galena's face. "Tovit knew this and that pig of a man I married turned you away, his own brother?"

Yosef gave a glum nod.

Galena stepped around him and hurried to Miryam slumped over on the donkey's back, hugging her swollen abdomen. "Miryam, you are a member of this family, my sister by marriage. Forget about what Tovit said, I will see to it that you receive the care you need."

The two women conversed in a low voice as Galena shot questions at her. When she'd learned all there was to know about Miryam's condition, she said, "Let me know when your next pain begins. I want to gauge how close you are."

Miryam motioned to her a short time later and Galena placed the flat of her hand on Miryam's belly. When the contraction ended, she pointed to a wooden chair in the yard and ordered Yosef to pull it over beside the donkey. She helped Miryam down and eased her into the chair. Promising to handle everything, she left them there and rushed back inside.

They could hear her in the house shouting commands as she marshaled the family into action. She grouped the children around her. "We must all help the wife of your Uncle Yosef. This is a special night for her." She grinned as her eyes moved from one to another. "By morning we will have a new baby in our family."

She sent the oldest boy into the cave-like stable that adjoined the house with instructions to move the animals out and tether them at a neighbor's. "Take your uncle's animal as well. The donkey will remember you and do as you command," she called after him.

Galena sent the oldest girl racing away into the night to find the midwife and bring her back. She formed the remaining children into a cleaning brigade and put them to work as the stable emptied. She told one boy to clean the stalls, and sent the two littler ones to sweep out the side of the barn where they stored feed.

Tovit came into the room as the youngsters scurried away, brooms in hand. "Everyone's working, what do you want me to do?"

Galena glared at him. "Go drown yourself in a well."

Leaving him with his mouth gaping, Galena spun on her heel and marched off. She went out to the stable to inspect the children's progress, barked more orders, and set her oldest son to strewing clean straw over the floor the children had swept.

Yosef moved the chair into the stable while Galena gathered blankets and pillows for a makeshift bed. She set up a room for Miryam in the back corner of the stable, and lit the lamps hanging from the posts. Their flames cast a warm orange glow over the makeshift birthing room.

Watching Miryam sink into the straw reminded Galena of a hen settling into her nest. "Well, what do you think?"

"I cannot imagine any place better," Miryam said. Here is where my child will be born, Miryam thought as she offered a silent prayer of thanksgiving.

Smiling for the first time, Yosef sat beside her on the straw and took her hand in his.

Miryam turned to speak, but stopped when a contraction started. She instantly shifted her breathing to short pants as the midwife in Nazareth had advised. As her travail continued, Miryam clamped down on Yosef's fingers with more strength than he ever imagined her having.

When the pain finally abated, Miryam sank back onto the pillows and closed her eyes. Galena mopped beads of sweat from her forehead. Putting the rag aside, she pointed a finger at Yosef. "You may stay for now, but if I say leave, you *will* go."

Before he could reply, Galena's oldest daughter returned to announce that the midwife was on her way.

Although fatigued, Miryam clasped her hands and gazed upward. She smiled and whispered, "Only you know how much I look forward to holding your miraculous child in my arms."

Yosef's fears melted away when he saw the joyful radiance on Miryam's face. Despite the setbacks and disappointments, he knew a protective hand had shepherded them to this place of security. He reached for her fingers and they shared a tired, but grateful sigh. When she glanced over at him he felt the confident trust in Miryam's eyes and she read the quiet strength in his.

— THE END —

Writer's Notes

People often choose fiction for entertainment, not what they can learn from it. However, besides the factual data that an author weaves into the story, we also gain new insights from the actions and reactions of the characters themselves. As the writer of *Road to Bethlehem*, I sincerely hope you found it entertaining, educational, and inspiring.

The Need for Accuracy in Fiction

No one can depict day-to-day life in a particular time and place without first developing a thorough understanding of that era. To me, accuracy is of paramount importance. This book, and the entire Seeds of Christianity Series which follows it, are as Biblically and historically accurate as I could make them. As a novelist, I exploit the gaps and omissions in the record, filling them in with logical details and consequences.

Sources of Information

The records we have of Joseph, Mary and their parents and family are, to put it simply, sparse at best. We're all familiar with the division of the Bible into the three synoptic Gospels on one side and the Gospel of John on the other. There is a second way of dividing them based on who provides a birth narrative and who doesn't. Here, the Gospels divide two and two with Mark and John omitting a birth narrative, and Luke and Matthew providing one.

And we can glean precious little from Matthew and Luke. Other than Elizabeth in Luke, neither of them mentions any of Mary's relatives. And the only genealogic information we have about Joseph is the name of his father, which is found in Matthew.

Most of what we *know* comes from tradition, that is, non-Biblical sources. For instance, the name of Mary's parents as well as a birth and infant narrative comes to us in the *Protoevangelium of James*, also known as *The Infancy Gospel of James*. While the title implies that it is the first Gospel, it references both Luke and

Matthew and is generally dated to the Third Century, long after the other Gospels were written. I used the names of Anna and Joachim because history gives us no others. However, the *Protoevangelium* describes Joachim as extremely wealthy, which hardly fits with his daughter marrying a somewhat lowly carpenter.

I also consulted several other sources of what might be called *private revelation*. Here are two: Anne Catherine Emmerich, a German nun and mystic who was born in1774 and died in 1824. She left transcriptions of her visions. I also read significant portions of Maria Valtorta's 4,200 page book, *The Gospel as Revealed to Me*. Also a mystic, this Italian laywoman lived from 1897 to 1961. Interestingly, both women were bed-ridden for much of their lives. While both left pious works behind, I found nothing so compelling in them that it led me in a new and different direction.

Why We Almost Titled the Book, *Journeys*.

The working title, *Journeys*, referenced the multiple trips both Mary and Joseph made back and forth between Galilee and Judea. The extent of their travels only became apparent to me when I overlaid the calendar of the Jewish pilgrim festivals with the Biblical narrative. There are some people who will insist that Jesus wasn't born on December 25th and all of this is merely a construct to accommodate pagan solstice celebrations, etc. I address those arguments in my nonfiction book, *All Things Christmas*. It's available through Amazon in both digital and print editions.

For now, let's just use the traditional dates assigned to the Feast of the Annunciation, (Gabriel coming to Mary in Nazareth), and the celebration of the birth of Jesus nine months later. *Pesach, Shavu'ot* and *Sukkoth* are movable feasts just like Easter. The date of both the Annunciation and Christmas are, of course, *fixed*.

Overlaying the one on the other, we find that Mary no sooner returns from celebrating the Passover in Jerusalem and Gabriel is knocking on her door. Luke tells us that Mary *"arose and went with haste into the hill country, to a city of Judah..."* She's there maybe six weeks and it's time for *Shavu'ot*.

John the Baptist is born about a month after her family returns home without her. Mary would have been gone 3 months plus an additional three weeks for the circumcision and travel both ways. Recall that when Gabriel mentions Elizabeth, he tells Mary, *"and this is the sixth month for her who was called barren..."* So Mary gets back home around mid July and is four months pregnant. Note, I'm allowing for travel time.

After resolving the issue of this unexpected event, she and Joseph marry. They settle in for no more than a couple of months and they're heading back to Jerusalem for the feast of *Sukkoth*. They return home for maybe 6 weeks, Caesar announces the census, and off they go to Bethlehem. And we think our schedules are hectic.

Mary and Elizabeth's Relationship

A cousin is the child of one of your parent's siblings. Is it possible to have a cousin who is nearly as old as a parent? Yes. A simple example: A person, whom we'll call Benjamin, has a sibling, Rueben, who is 16 years older. Rueben's first child is born when Benjamin is 4. Meanwhile, Benjamin is 36 years old when his last child is born. In this example, these cousins are 32 years apart.

Now let's return to Elizabeth and Mary. Elizabeth is obviously the older cousin, making Mary the younger cousin by default. Here's where things get a bit sticky. Luke takes pains to emphasize Elizabeth's old age.

In our earlier example, the cousins were 32 years apart. The prevailing assumption is that Mary was probably around sixteen or seventeen years of age when Jesus was born. A 16 year-old Mary and a 32 year spread, gives us a 48-year-old Elizabeth. This is, at best, only marginally workable. At 48 Elizabeth is hardly *advanced in years* as Luke so discretely puts it.

There is another, and to my mind, more acceptable possibility. Let's suppose that Mary's *mother* and Elizabeth are first cousins. Now that first born sibling who had a child early on and the last child born to the youngest sibling stuff all goes away. Anna and Joachim have one child, Mary. This would make Mary and Elizabeth *first cousins once removed.* I can't imagine anyone introducing a person by saying, "I'd like you to meet my first cousin once removed." We'd simply say, "This is my cousin."

Mary and Joseph's Relationship

I sincerely hope I didn't disturb readers by the obvious romantic feelings Mary and Joseph have for each other and their acts of affection. In defense, I would first point out that the two of them were betrothed *before* the appearance of the angel Gabriel. One could assume all marriages of that era were arranged and therefore romance never entered the picture...sort of like the marvelous scene from *Fiddler on the Roof* where Tevye asks his wife, Golde, over and over, "*Do you love me?*"

I find nothing problematic about a Mary and Joseph who are genuinely in love. This, of course, leads us into the issue of Joseph's age and the *brothers and sisters* of Jesus mentioned in the Gospels. The Eastern tradition assumes Joseph was an elderly widower who sought a housekeeper and step-mother for his children rather than the traditional marital relationship. You'll see many paintings that depict Joseph as elderly. This most likely developed as a way to support the belief in Mary's perpetual virginity. In other words, rather than portray Joseph as holy and chaste, you simply make him so old he doesn't give a hoot about that stuff anymore. Personally, I prefer the first option, that he deserves respect as a *holy and chaste* man.

For those who are interested, both the age of Joseph and the siblings of Jesus are discussed in greater detail in the chapter, *Three Views of St. Joseph*, in my book, *All Things Christmas, The History and Traditions of Advent and Christmas*. http://www.amazon.com/dp/B004DNWIHI

The Trip to Bethlehem for the Census

The *Great Migration* from Judea to portions of Galilee during the reign of Hasmonean ruler, Alexander Jannaeus, is a well documented. I introduced it because I believe it might have had some bearing on who had to go to Bethlehem and who didn't. Obviously Joseph had to return to Bethlehem because that was where he was born. But what about someone who'd been in Galilee for three or four generations?

Imagine how disruptive this would have been. Even in the First Century there was a large and widely dispersed Diaspora. For the sake of argument, we'll agree that anyone living within the original boundaries of Israel had to return to their ancestral home. What about those who lived elsewhere in the Roman Empire? Alexandria had a Jewish population that rivaled Jerusalem. Antioch had a large Jewish Quarter as did Rome. Were all of these people really expected to go home to Israel for the census?

Many Jews lived beyond the borders of the Roman Empire. A large contingent remained behind in Babylon instead of returning to rebuild the Temple. There are even records of a Jewish enclave in India.

Algum Wood and the Illusive Ophir

The uses and characteristics of algum wood align nicely with what we now call sandalwood. Ophir, meanwhile, is alternately said to have been somewhere in modern Africa or India. What really clinches it for me is the fact that algum wood came by boat via the Red Sea. The Romans had well established trade routes to India and product was handled pretty much the way Joseph describes it in the book. Spice and incense were two of the primary trade goods. Sandalwood is used for, among other things, incense. The tree is also native to India.

Beth HaKerem

Ancient records indicate that the village of Beth HaKerem has a long and storied existence dating back to the Bronze Age.

Mentioned by both Nehemiah and Jeremiah, it was the site of an ancient reservoir. Archaeological digs have discovered the remains of oil presses and *mikvahs*, pools for ritual cleansing. Because it is the city of John the Baptist's birth, it is home to several large churches, among them The Church of John the Baptist and The Church of the Visitation. What was an independent village 2,000 years ago has now become a suburb of greater Jerusalem known as Ein Kerem.

The Mah Nistanah

In Exodus 12:25-27 the Jews are told to keep the Passover for all time as a memorial and to tell their children its meaning. This command is fulfilled to this day with the *Four Questions*. This is an important part of the Seder meal and the questions are typically delegated to the youngest child. The questions are chanted and answered in Hebrew. The first word of the sequence, *Why is this night different from all other nights?* is *Mah nishtanah*. In *Road to Bethlehem*, Shoshanna, a Down syndrome child, sings the opening and the four questions that follow:

1. On all other nights, we eat either unleavened or leavened bread, but tonight we eat only unleavened bread?

2. On all other nights, we eat all kinds of vegetables, but tonight, we eat only bitter herbs?

3. On all other nights, we do not dip [our food] even once, but tonight we dip twice?

4. On all other nights, we eat either sitting or reclining, but tonight we only recline?

Harmonia's Necklace

I am often amazed at the surreptitious way characters and plotlines emerge. Case in point, I introduced Harmonia as a sympathetic woman who provided the assistance Miryam so badly needed. She was, if you will, heaven sent. I did this not knowing she would turn out to be a widow who had lost a child. The necklace grew out of the idea of her viewing Miryam as a surrogate daughter.

When naming a character or creating a symbol such as the necklace, I try to have some underlying rationale. The concept of birthstones is said to have originated with Aaron's breastplate with its 12 stones, one for each tribe. Mary's birth appears in September on the liturgical calendar. Therefore, it seemed appropriate to choose the birthstone for September, Sapphire, for Harmonia's necklace.

The term "Sapphire" appears many times in the Bible. The Roman historian, Pliny the Elder, describes the *sapphiros* of the Bible as "refulgent with spots like gold. It is also of an azure color...the best kind coming from Media. In no case, however, is this stone transparent." This more accurately describes what we know today as *lapis lazuli*, not the sapphire of modern times. We now also know the *gold* Pliny mentions is actually pyrite. By coincidence, Lapis Lazuli is considered the stone of truth and friendship.

Treading in the Garden of Good and Evil

Though subtle, evil definitely stalks Miryam. It seems quite reasonable to assume that Satan would have done all he could to undo the Incarnation in any way he could.

Why was the young man who tried to attack Miryam named Cerberus? In Greek mythology, Cerberus guards the gate to the underworld. He is sometimes depicted as a three-headed dog with a serpent's tail, a mane of snakes, and a lion's claws. The name works well for someone recruited by the devil to harm the unborn Christ child.

Having failed in his first attempt, it's easy to imagine Satan tempting Joseph to have Mary stoned rather than simply *put her away*, as some translations term it. In the book, the angel of his dream not only appears to assure Joseph that he should wed Mary, he also spells out in ways Joseph would understand what his role and relationship with her will be.

When both of Satan's attempts failed, he tried to derail the process a third time by having Herod search out and try to kill the child. Left with few alternatives, the devil then waited 33 years to tempt Christ in the desert. There's no doubt in my mind that he finally struck pay dirt with the High Priest and his cronies, though this success was short lived.

On the side of goodness, we find the aptly named Harmonia, an angel of mercy, who steps in at an opportune time to rescue Miryam from clear and present danger.

Peace and Blessings,

September 8, 2015
The Feast of the Nativity of the Blessed Virgin Mary

WITNESS — BOOK ONE

An epic tale of love lost and love found

Rivkah, a young shepherdess, accompanies her father to Bethlehem where, with Mary's help, she holds her the newborn Christ child. But Mary, Joseph and Jesus soon go away to Egypt. She meets stranger from the East who've followed a star and Herod's soldiers begin killing the children of her village.

Then her intended, Shemu'el, is dragged away into slavery. Divided by fate, united by love, these two young people grow to separate adulthood, each with their dreams and desires unfulfilled. Meanwhile, the world of Rome moves inexorably on. False messiahs rise and fall with fatal consequences.

Rivkah eventually marries and raises a family. Life is good until the day she encounters Jesus a final time... on his way to crucifixion. She follows and this time, as they take him from the cross, it's Rivkah who helps Mary hold her son. Biblically and historically accurate.

DISCIPLE — BOOK TWO

The Seeds of Christianity find Fertile Soil

Rivkah and her family convert to the Way of Yeshua. Unable to survive in their home settlement, they move to Jerusalem. Increasing persecution there again forces them out. They head for Antioch with Simon Peter to establish the Church there.

Experience life in the early Church as the first Christians struggle to live out the teachings of Yeshua in an often hostile environment. Sit beside the twelve apostles as they partition the world and begin their mission of preaching and teaching. Encounter Saul of Tarsus, the scourge of the early Church and Stephen, the first to die for his faith

Stand beside Channah as she watches a mob stone the man she loves. Meet Pavlos of Antioch, the mute giant whose actions speak louder than words, and whose innate goodness created a ministry to the weak and helpless. Weep for Eleana, a young woman who was savagely attacked by a Roman soldier and now must decide whether to keep the child that is surely his.

APOSTLE — BOOK THREE

The Church at Antioch comes into its own.

Tensions surface as the number of non-Jewish converts rises. Barnabas goes to Tarsus and returns with Paul, but Rivkah's daughter, Channah, opposes his new role. This saga of the Early Church takes a troubling turn when Rivkah's youngest son leaves home and adopts a pagan lifestyle.

Meanwhile, Antioch trembles in the grip of a ruthless serial killer. While Pavlos roams the streets searching for him, Shemu'el fears he already knows the killer's identity.

The Emperor, Claudius, expels all Jews from Rome, ending Simon Peter's ministry there. Meanwhile, the beloved disciple, Yohan, has relocated to Ephesus for Miryam's protection. He brings Shemu'el a new convert named Ignatius and asks him to mentor the young man. Though surrounded by chaos, the church in Antioch grows in size and influence under Shemu'el's competent leadership. Biblically and historically accurate.

MARTYR — BOOK FOUR
The Seeds of Christianity goes to Rome

Claudius is gone and Nero now wears the crown. Jews are returning to Rome meaning Simon Peter can resume his missionary work there.

Rivkah and her family set sail for Rome just as a revolt breaks out in Britannia. Led by Queen Boaddicea of the Iceni, she aims to wrest the Province from Roman hands. A huge conflagration leaves most of Rome in ashes. When voices rise in the street accusing Nero being the incendiary, he searches for a scapegoat. Nero's wife, Poppea, still smarting from Atticus' rejection of her advances, suggests he blame the Christians. She realizes too late that like Pandora, she has unleashed a demon she cannot control.

The Christians construct the first catacomb and its niches quickly fill as more and more believers are slain for their faith. As their numbers climb, Shemu'el realizes they have a traitor in their midst. But how can he identify this false Christian who's selling out his friends to save his own skin?